S I S T E R S   O F   I N T E R M E N T

SISTERS OF INTERMENT

stories by gary bigelow

■ red crane books

santa fe

First Edition
Printed in the United States of America
Illustrations and graphics by Gary Bigelow
Book design and production by Beverly Miller Atwater

Dedication

For
Catherine

Library of Congress Cataloging-in-Publication Data
Bigelow, Gary

Sisters of Interment : stories by / Gary Bigelow.
p.   cm.
ISBN 1-878610-67-8
1. United States—Social life and customs—20th century—Fiction.
2. City and town life—United States—Fiction.
I. Title.
PS3552.I418S5   1998
813'.54—dc21
98-36273
CIP

RED CRANE BOOKS
2008 B Rosina Street
Santa Fe, New Mexico 87505
http://www.redcrane.com
email: publish@redcrane.com

■ ACKNOWLEDGMENTS

I would like to express my sincerest gratitude to those who have supported, encouraged and believed in these stories: Michael and Marianne O'Shaughnessy, Beverly Miller Atwater, Daniel Kosharek and Norma Belenchia. Special thanks to my new friend and editor, Cindy Barrilleaux and her husband, Steve. A special debt is also owed to my family for their many sacrifices over the years.

The Allegöry Falls Chaptër of the James Joycë Litëraky Socïety

(a stylistic tribute to James Joyce)

 Nestled between Woolworth's and the Moxie Theater on Hatch Street was a narrow, nineteenth-century storefront. The antique gold Gothic lettering on its single, frosted-paned window read Dedalus Books.

The blink-of-an-eye-and-you've-missed-it shop was owned by a shy young woman with auburn hair, hazel eyes and a complexion as creamy and smooth as if it had never been touched by the summer's sun. She wore peasant dresses that stopped just past mid-calf rustling like quaking Aspen when she walked. Around her neck hung a simple, heart-shaped gold locket. Passers-by could see her bent over the counter on a tall stool or bustling about the shop dusting the bookshelves that reached from the worn wooden floor to the stucco swirl patterns on the ceiling. Every Friday, just before closing, she placed a calligraphied placard in the window. It read: Meeting of the Allegory Falls Chapter of the James Joyce Literary Society, Saturday Evening, 7:30 p.m., at 30½ Hatch Street.

Donovan Magruder happened by the shop one winter's afternoon after working his shift at Haig's Bar. He was running an errand for his Aunt Clare, and noticed the sign propped against a stack of John Grisham bestsellers in the storefront window. He had never heard of the James Joyce Literary Society, let alone the existence of a local chapter, but he didn't have time to enter the shop and ask for more information from the woman he could faintly see through the shop's heavy glass door.

The next morning after breakfast with his aunt, Donovan returned to his room on the top floor of the boarding house and looked out at the falling snow that clung precariously to the eaves. It was a cold, grey Saturday, and despite Aunt Clare's Belgian waffles and boiled coffee, the unmade Murphy bed looked warm and inviting. Donovan crossed the creaky wood floor to the bookcase nestled in the corner next to the bed and looked at the books scattered on the shelves. It had been some time since he had dusted the dog-eared pages of Joyce's books. Taking one at random, Donovan climbed into his spongy bed and began re-reading A *Portrait of the Artist as a Young Man*. The rest of the morning he read the lines that were so familiar to him. What was it about Joyce, he pondered, glancing out the window at the falling snow, that made each rereading reveal something entirely new? Turning a page, he suddenly remembered the placard in the window of the bookshop. A James Joyce Literary Society in Allegory Falls? Donovan could not resist the pull of the invitation.

———

At 7:20 p.m., Donovan stood in front of the bookstore at 30 Hatch Street, looking for the entrance to 30½. There was no other door on that half-block, no door within a doorway, so he wandered down the faintly lit alley, through the clouds of steam rising from Caffrey's Dry Cleaners. He came to a heavy wooden delivery door with a peephole the size of a bread slice. A small bulb hung over the entrance and revealed the numbers 30½ carelessly painted and run together.

Donovan knocked on the door lightly. Kawlap. Kawlunk. Kawlake. Nervously looking about to see if anyone was watching him, he knocked again. Finally, he heard the latch on the peephole turn and saw the young woman he had seen through the window of Dedalus Books.

–Password? she politely asked.

–Password? What password?

–THE password, she added, matter-of-factly.

–There's a password? Donovan's eyebrows knitted together. But this is supposed to be a literary society.

    –It doesn't matter. You have to use the correct password, she emphatically stated. Joyce demanded it.

    –But I don't know the password.

    –Guess then, she answered softly, smiling.

    –Guess? This is absurd.

    –But it's the only way of being admitted.

    –Are you sure that Joyce would have wanted it this way?

    –Absolutely. Haven't you read *Ulysses* and *Finnegan's Wake*?

    –Yes, some time ago, but what does that have to do with the password? I'm not sure I completely understood *Finnegan's Wake*, anyway.

    –Joyce's wife, Nora, once asked him why he didn't write books people could read. But be that as it may, perhaps you should re-read it.

    –I'm confused—so, if I guess and I'm wrong...Donovan

hesitated.

 –Yes, she spritely responded. You won't be admitted. But you can guess again.

 –How many guesses do I get? asked Donovan, making patterns in the snow with his feet.

 –As many as you like or that I have patience for tonight or any other night, should you decide to return.

 –This is strange. Donovan nervously chuckled and muttered *password* under his breath.

 –That's the way it has to be. The James Joyce Literary Society cannot allow just anyone admittance.

 –Why would Joyce care? One would think...that..., stammered Donovan.

 –Oh, but he did. It's written into the original charter. Joyce was a stickler for details, you know. Details, details, details.

 –Charter? Details? The cold nipped at Donovan's fingertips inside the lined pockets of his jacket. He leaned closer to the tiny door with a puzzled look.

 –All societies have charters.

 –This is unbelievable. Why—

The peep door shut. Donovan stared in disbelief before it sharply reopened.

 –It's right here, in black and white. She held a thick, bound document to the tiny window. Donovan squinted, trying to read the script in the darkness of the alley. This was penned by Joyce himself in 1913 after he failed to get the *Dubliners* published a year earlier.

 –I have never heard of anything like that, and I know something about Joyce.

 –Well, I'm afraid you don't know everything. She began to shut the small door.

 –No, wait, please, Donovan replied, hurriedly. I said I was skeptical, but I didn't say I wasn't interested.

 –Are you going to guess then? she asked.

 –Sure, I suppose so. By the way, what's your name?

–Sure…suppose…maybe?? That doesn't speak of much interest. Gillian Fitzpatrick, and yours? she asked.

–That's a nice name. I'm Donovan Magruder. Alright then, give me a minute to think.

–Don't take too long, time's wasting, Donovan Magruder.

–Dedalus? he blurted. The word crystallized in the night air.

–Not even close, she said, giving a faint chuckle as she shut the peephole.

Donovan, not easily dissuaded, knocked again. Gillian opened the tiny, hinged door, and flashed her half-hidden smile.

–Ulysses? Donovan asked, wide-eyed.

–Ha! she laughed. Everyone guesses that at one time or another. That's as predictable as Dedalus. Gillian shut the door rapidly.

As fast as he heard the catch fall, Donovan knocked on the door and the latch turned, revealing Gillian's twinkling eyes once more.

–Why can't I just keep guessing without having to wear out my knuckles on this door? Donovan asked, another guess perched on his lips.

–It's against the charter rules, she replied briskly.

–Rules? Why?

–To make sure the person wanting admittance is serious.

–Doesn't it look like I'm serious? asked Donovan. I'm still here. And what does shutting the—

–So you are, and if you are, you'll knock again. They all say that at one time or another, as well. It's as predictable as guessing Ulysses, she brightly stated.

–All?

–The others who have tried and failed before you. Did you think you're the only one to try?

–You mean others…, began Donovan, taking a deep breath.

–Yes, replied Gillian, although no one has succeeded up to this point in time.

–No one?

–Not here. It's almost as if they have to be touched by the hand of Joyce himself.

–Sounds rather mystical and pompous to me. How can you have a James Joyce Literary Society with so few members, and how is it that you are the sole member of this particular chapter?

–Firstly, Joyce wanted it that way. It was his way of preserving the integrity of his work. And there's nothing pompous or mystical about it. Mythical, undoubtedly. Secondly, I head this chapter because I was admitted to a chapter in Chicago some years ago. By society rules, once a person gains admission, the previous member must seek out a place where no James Joyce Literary Society is established. Once I initiated a new member, I was obligated to seek out a new locale. So I came to Allegory Falls.

–What if you never admit anyone during your lifetime?

–That will never happen, Gillian said confidently. That will never happen.

–Why? he asked.

–So many questions, she replied. There is always someone who desires admission and by sheer will and knowledge, or guessing, as you put it, enters the society. Joyce would not have had it any other way, nor would he have chosen a password that no one seriously trying could guess.

–So, how long did it take Joyce to commission someone? And where did they go?

–Almost ten years after he wrote the charter. It was in 1922, after *Ulysses* was published. Dublin.

–Hmm, intoned Donovan. Likely place…So, may I guess again?

–If you like, but this is the last time for this week. You can come back next Saturday, if you want, and try again but this is your last time tonight. I am getting tired and very cold.

–You mean I can't come into your shop and guess?

–No, that is strictly forbidden, Gillian said.

–I know—Joyce wouldn't have wanted it that way.

–Exactly! Now you're getting it.

–Why are these meetings held on Saturdays? Donovan asked.

–You are full of questions, aren't you? If you must know, that is the day of the week Joyce and Nora, his lovely wife, left Ireland for a life of exile on the continent, and that is the day he chose, quite symbolically, to hold the meetings.

–I didn't know that detail of his life.

–Many do not. Now, are you going to guess again or do I have to, not out of rudeness mind you, shut the door?

Donovan stood and concentrated. The flakes of snow fell silently and blanketed his head.

–You are thinking too much again, said Gillian, impatiently.

Donovan's mind was awash with Joyce. The stories, the characters, the settings, the lines, the cacophony of words sped through his mind. How could he possibly guess a password created by the master of word games who boasted the difficulty of his work? Out of the thousands and even hundreds of thousands of possible words, what could it be? He remembered Joyce's question—What kind of liberation would it be to forsake an absurdity that is logical and coherent and to embrace one illogical and incoherent? Donovan's head throbbed from the strain.

–Well? Gillian took hold of the small door and toyed with the latch.

–Baby Tuckoo, blurted Donovan. Yes, Baby Tuckoo, that nicens little boy who met that moocow once upon a time and a very good time it was, is my guess.

–A valiant effort and one that I have never heard before, Gillian said, smiling. She closed the peephole door and gave the latch a quick flick.

Donovan stood thoroughly perplexed before the heavy door as the snow began falling faster. He turned and walked briskly home, confused but confident that he could choose the right password. But what would that mean? Would he have to leave Allegory Falls, a place he loved so much? Did he want to take that risk? The question tugged at Donovan's spirit as he trudged homeward.

At 7:20 p.m., on a Saturday weeks after his initial visit, Donovan anxiously approached the door and knocked again. Thwap. Thwap. Gillian did not answer on the first knock, so he repeated the ritual.

    –Donovan! Back again, I see, said Gillian cheerfully.

    –Yes. And how are you this week?

    –Fine, thank you. Are you ready to try again?

    –I think so, replied Donovan with a deep sigh. I've been thinking how this may affect my life once I am admitted. I mean, I don't want to leave. So…

    –But you haven't been admitted yet. And that is a choice you have to make, but then again you may never commission anyone. I've only had two others before you. Seems Allegory Falls is not a mecca for Joyce fanatics.

    –Yes, that's true, Donovan replied, placing his trembling fingers against the weathered door.

    –Ready to try? Gillian asked.

Donovan took his time answering; Gillian waited patiently.

–Bloody?

–Why did you choose that word? Gillian asked, cocking her head to one side and leaning closer to the tiny door. Donovan immediately thought he might have chosen the right word.

–I was thinking of how Joyce was faced with the prospect of having that word edited out of his early work and his belief that a writer should oppose any alteration of his work. Is that…?

–That's true, but unfortunately, it is not the correct word, although it's rumored within the society that Joyce gave it serious consideration. Gillian shut the small viewing door.

Donovan was exasperated, but he knocked again. Tap. Tap.

–I knew you wouldn't leave. I can tell that you are more serious than the others who have sought entrance to the society. They gave up after a few uncalculated guesses. One person did return and set fire to all of Joyce's work, right where you are standing.

–What sacrilege! Donovan said, trying to ingratiate himself.

–Yes, I thought so too. And they were first editions too! To think of all the Joyce books that have been burned over the years…

–What would Joyce have thought? stated Donovan.

–He would have bloody well put the culprit's teeth down his throat, she replied with a laugh.

–Perhaps, Donovan smiled back at her. That line has a ring of familiarity.

–It's from the story about the boarding house in the *Dubliners*.

–That's right, I remember now! Jack shouted that line, Donovan replied enthusiastically.

–Yes. It appears you know Joyce's works well. You must have been studying them quite religiously these past weeks.

–I have.

–Ready to try again? Gillian asked.

Donovan didn't reply—his mind had gone totally blank. Gillian recognized the look and waited silently. Suddenly Donovan beamed and the dim light of the snowy alley briefly seemed to intensify.

—Sraid Mabbot! He shouted, dancing in a circle outside the door. The password is Sraid Mabbot!

—So, asked Gillian, as Donovan ducked clumsily through the threshold of the Allegory Falls Chapter of the James Joyce Literary Society. You should be commended. Many spend months, even years knocking at the doors of the society. What finally brought you to choose those words?

—Well, I was feeling light in the head from all the guessing. Then I remembered a passage in *Ulysses*. It was the only time Joyce ever made mention of a password, Donovan said excitedly.

—I knew, from the first time I laid eyes on you, that you were to be the next member. Gillian closed the door on the cold alley where Donovan's footprints lay glazed in the snow.

Donovan looked at his new surroundings. It was a claustrophobic room, once used for storage, with only a small, ratty, dank couch. A little lamp with a beige shade stood on an end table, its light reflecting on an amateurish oil portrait of Joyce, obviously painted from the photograph of Joyce wearing his hat cocked back on his head. There was a small table with a Royal typewriter next to a bookcase of Joyce's works. A gaudy sheet of notepaper was in the typewriter. Gillian led Donovan to the sofa. They sat at opposite ends, and discussed Donovan's initiation.

A knock came on the door. It had been quite some time since Donovan remembered what it had been like for him when he first knocked on that door. He thought fondly of Gillian now that she was gone. As he approached the door, he remembered a few lines from Joyce: I *do not fear to be alone. And I am not afraid to make a mistake, even a great mistake, a lifelong mistake, and perhaps as long as eternity too.* Just as Gillian had done, and according to the Charter that Joyce had brought forth with his own hand, Donovan waited for a second knock before reaching for the latch on the peephole of the door tucked down the alley behind Dedalus Books.

—Password? Donovan asked, peering through the small eye of the door.

 On a cool, rainy day Pete Gentile snuggled the brass rail of Haig's Bar with chilled toes curled in his heavy, black oxfords. A sanguine man with a pleasant, narrow face, bright eyes the color of hand-rubbed mahogany and an inquisitive smile, Pete wore his trademark Eisenhower jacket, the pockets stuffed with business cards, magazine clippings and notes that he constantly sorted through to plot his next sales pitch. Pete's head was always in the clouds, filled with grandiose dreams.

Pete was perched on the bar stool, slumped over the counter like a gargoyle. In front of him sat a near-full glass of beer, whose foamy head had crystalized in an interlocking pattern on the inside of the glass. Donovan, an expert at spotting stale glasses of beer and what generally accompanies them, moved down the bar to Pete.

"I'm ruined," Pete said in a precise voice. "This time I've really gone and done it."

"Aw, things can't be that bad," said Donovan, knowing Pete was nowhere near the entrepreneur he claimed to be. "What's wrong? I've never seen you down like this before. You've always bounced back when things haven't gone well." He wiped the bar with a pungent, stale rag.

"I was going through my mail a few months ago and spotted this letter addressed to Occupant." Pete paused and took a sip from his glass. "I opened the letter as soon as I entered the house. It was from an Omega, Inc., out of Los Angeles. I had never heard of them before, but their logo really put the hook into me. It was red and black and in small glossy print read: Worms of the World Unite."

Donovan placed a fresh glass in front of Pete, who went on, "Omega was one of those new enviro-tech companies involved with alternative measures for controlling pollution and sewage. They were also heavily involved in agribusiness, fertilizers and vermiculture. That's what interested me right away, living here next to so much agriculture."

"That sounds reasonable so far," Donovan said. "And?"

"Exactly. Do you know the capacity of the genus *Lumbricus* to recycle garbage and produce natural fertilizer from its castings?" Pete asked enthusiastically.

"No," said Donovan, playing into Pete's hands, "but I bet it's a lot."

"I'll say. Omega predicted that by the year 2013, worms would be used to consume 45 percent of the world's garbage and produce 30-some percent of its fertilizer. That's an amazing statistic when you think about it."

"That's a lot of worms, Pete." Donovan tried to suppress his urge to laugh. He'd never heard of worms being used for anything but fishing, and aerating Aunt Clare's flower beds. She swore by them for enriching the black earth beneath her lupines and roses, mums and asters. On occasion, Donovan had heard her talking to them as she dug her beds, quickly covering the ones she accidently unearthed. Fishing and flower beds, maybe—but half the world's garbage?

Pete went on to explain that Omega was listed on the New York Stock Exchange and that they were looking for serious investors. Donovan fought back the image of Pete as a worm rancher by remembering Pete's past efforts to hit "the big one," as Pete always put it.

After finishing high school in the late '50s, Pete embarked on his ill-fated career in sales. His first great hope was the Veg-a-Matic

but, as Aunt Clare said when she bought one, "it would never replace a good sharp knife."

Pete next tried to make his fortune peddling tin siding. After a hailstorm made the Fourth Street neighborhood sound like a combat zone and left the front of Joe Stuckey's house as pitted as the surface of the moon, word quickly spread that tin siding was not all it claimed to be.

But Pete always found another scheme to strike it rich. It was 1964 when Pete mortgaged the boarding house his mother had left him when she died the year before. He invested all the money into the Range of the Future—The Caloric 75, which featured an overhead broiler, removable oven door, and the latest innovation: a self-cleaning oven. Pete had seen a commercial for the range one night on the *Ozzie and Harriet Show,* and immediately began scheming. He was convinced the self-cleaning oven would open every door in Allegory Falls to him and his Caloric 75, somehow forgetting that he had thought the same of his earlier ventures. So he sank all his money into thirty-three white enameled ranges at a one-time, low introductory price, overlooking the non-refundable, no-return clause. Dollar signs flickered in Pete's eyes like the lights of Main Street on a Saturday night as he surveyed the ranges neatly aligned in rows in his garage.

The course of Pete's life may have been different had it not been for another small detail that he overlooked in his haste. Mrs. Brotsky was the first to order a Caloric 75 from him, convinced that the self-cleaning feature would give her more time with her six children, ages two through nine, plus another one on the way. Pete wheeled the range through her back door, removed her old four-burner electric, and happily backed the Caloric 75 into place.

"You're gonna love this," said Pete, as Mrs. Brotsky and her brood stood near and watched him install it. A few minutes later he was writing her a check and re-installing the old electric. The Caloric 75, regrettably, was designed for natural gas, and it would be seventeen years before gas lines reached Allegory Falls. By then the Caloric 75 was obsolete. It took nearly as many years for him to unload the appliances in nearby towns. The house Pete had mortgaged was put on the auction block a year later and became Magruder's Boarding House. Aunt Clare let Pete stay on for a year to help him get back on his feet. He got a job working part time as a postal clerk, which gave him endless junk mail to search through for his next big opportunity.

Pete's voice broke through Donovan's reverie. "I decided to invest in Omega that very moment, and to start my own worm business and sell fertilizer back to Omega. That way I wouldn't have to rely on anyone around here to buy anything," he said with some bitterness.

"You mean to tell me…"

"Yes. I invested everything I had and even borrowed some money."

"The bank let you do that?" asked Donovan.

"I had to put up my old Buick as collateral," he said, without any emotion in his voice. He struggled with each word to explain his new-found passion. "I spent hours building crates and filling them with soil and garbage. My basement and garage became mass-production zones. I even went as far as having business cards printed after watching Omega's stock prices rise in the *Wall Street Journal*." He reached into the pocket of his green flannel shirt and extracted a card, which he placed on the bar in front of Donovan. In raised black letters it read: Gentile Worm Works, Peter I. Gentile, Owner. "I was eventually going to expand my operation to a small farm."

"How is it that in a town of this size, no one knew of your enterprise?" asked Donovan as he stared at the card.

"Amazing, isn't it?" said Pete. "You know as well as I do it isn't easy keeping a secret in this town, but I wanted to prevent any competition."

"Claim jumpers, hey Pete?" responded Donovan, tongue-in-cheek.

"Sure, I guess. Half-a-million worms are surprisingly inconspicuous. I worked mostly at night, keeping out of sight."

"How did you manage to accumulate that many worms?" asked Donovan, pouring a beer for another customer.

"You'd be surprised how easy it is," droned Pete, as if he were a nineteenth-century cattle baron. "Most of the work, like I said, was done at night, with a gunny sack, flashlight and an electric prod. Brings 'em right up. Scores of 'em. They just hover in the grass, like the grass was plump, wavy hair. Pick 'em and plop 'em in the bag."

"Electric prod?" Donovan imagined Pete's pleasure in turning the copper rod into an electroconvulsive tool.

"I just plugged it into outdoor outlets or fuse boxes. I even made a special adapter for it," said Pete. "After I depleted my yard and the neighbors', I covered most of the yards in Allegory Falls. I collected garbage the same way, too, starting at the Cafe."

Donovan conjured up an image of worms suffering indigestion and diarrhea like the patrons of the Ranch Cafe. "No one ever caught you?"

"Oh, I had close calls, but I dressed in solid black, even had a black ski mask," answered Pete, twitching his fingers delicately together as if he were plucking a worm from its earthy home.

"What about dogs?"

"Hate to say it, but I installed a crude voltage regulator on my electric prod. It doubled really well as a stun gun."

"Did you ever—" began Donovan.

"Once, in one of your friend's yard. It hit my leg when I was fumbling in her flower bed. I was out for a good fifteen minutes," Pete winced, reaching for his glass.

Donovan pictured Pete among the flowers, the contents of his teeming gunny sack squirming for freedom as he lay unconscious. He couldn't stop himself from laughing. "So you actually—"

"I don't think it's funny," Pete interrupted, "but yeah, I guess I rustled worms."

Donovan looked at him straight-faced. "I'm sure no one will litigate."

"Doesn't matter. I'm ruined."

"I don't understand. What about the fertilizer? You can sell it to Omega."

"I have over a million worms and the numbers are rising as we speak," began Pete. "Prolific, they are. With their value and the amount of fertile soil they produce I should be wealthy by now. But Omega overextended themselves and the stock plummeted. Now the company is bankrupt and can't buy any of my fertilizer."

Donovan leaned across the bar. "There's nothing you can do?"

"Nothing. My stock is worthless. I could sell the castings around here, but the farmers and ranchers produce enough of their own. All I have are legions of hungry worms and mounds of fertilizer." Pete shook his legs to circulate the blood in his feet and stood up. "Thanks for listening, Donovan." He slowly crossed the room and exited through the glass door.

Donovan stared at Pete's business card for a moment before he tucked it into his jean's pocket. He shook his head, picked up the empty glass and gave the bar another swipe with his rag. "Now I've heard everything."

A week later, Pete bounced into Haig's. Donovan was cleaning the tables just before closing.

"You're up late," he said to Pete, whose face was aglow. "Did you just swallow the canary?" Pete sat on a stool while Donovan finished cleaning up. "So tell me why you're so happy. This is quite a turnaround from last week."

"I think I have found a solution to my problem," began Pete. "I was over to the next county and stopped in at the K-Mart. I began pitching the advantages of worm casting fertilizer to the garden and nursery manager." Pete paused, shuffling through his coat pockets.

"And?"

"And he liked it," smiled Pete, pulling out an order sheet and showing it to Donovan. "They'll buy as much as my worms can produce. Seems the weekend gardeners prefer it to manure compost."

"That's great, Pete. I knew you would find a way out of your predicament." Donovan patted him on the back as the two left the bar. After Donovan locked the door, Pete turned and hesitantly asked, "I was wondering if maybe you could help me out."

"Depends on what kind of help," hedged Donovan.

"Sacking, weighing and crating bags...it'd only be for a couple of days. After I get the initial shipments off, I can manage on my own."

"Sure, Pete," said Donovan with a smile. "I'd like to see your operation anyway."

As he walked toward Pete's house a couple of days later, Donovan saw a large mound in the backyard like the ancient burial mounds pictured in National Geographic. After tapping on the partially opened door and getting no answer, he entered the house and called out to Pete. There was no response, so he looked around. The kitchen was filled with plastic bags K-Mart had made specifically for Pete's worm castings. A partially filled bag sat near the sink, labeled Gentile's All-Natural Plant Food, 100% Worm Castings, A Gardener's Best Friend, with the K-Mart logo beneath. The sink was soiled from spilled castings, where Pete must have begun without him. A few of Pete's herd were slowly dying on the sun-drenched formica. "Must be out back," Donovan thought. He went out the screen door. "Pete!" he called over and over as he neared the mound.

Empty pine crate upon pine crate littered the yard, garage and house, some covered with earthy residue, and others with their earthy inhabitants still squirming about. Donovan searched everywhere for Pete and his miniature dachshund, Franklin, who should have been barking long before Donovan stepped through the gate, but they were nowhere to be found. As he wandered about, taking in the silent, fetid smell of earth and castings, and surveying the disarray, a protracted, cold shiver permeated his body. Donovan turned and began to run.

 "Did I just see—" began Donovan, as he came through the back door to find Aunt Clare staring out the kitchen window.

She smiled as she interrupted her nephew in mid-sentence. "That's right, dear. Mrs. Spanos paid me a visit this afternoon. One more quilt, one more piece of magic to work."

"I don't know why you give your quilts away if you think they are so special," said Donovan, wrinkling his face. "You should at least sell them, for all the effort you put into them."

"They're special quilts, dear," Aunt Clare replied, her reading spectacles reflecting light spots around the kitchen walls. "You can't put a price on everything in life, Donovan. It will affect the magic of them." She patted Donovan on the arm, as she returned to her sewing room adjoining the kitchen.

Aunt Clare was more than the proprietor of the local boarding house, more than a maker of home remedies, and more than one of the "sisters of interment," as Donovan had dubbed her friends. She was also the maker of quilts, and mind you, they were not your run-of-the-mill quilts. They were magic quilts. At least, that is what the people who visited her believed.

Aunt Clare's sewing room was also more than a day-room filled with odds and ends of fabrics, threads, an antique Singer sewing machine and two pitifully decaying manikins, pierced with pearlesque-headed hat pins she had procured when the Mode-O-Day apparel shop went out of business. This was Aunt Clare's "office," where she counseled her clients at a small, round cherry table covered with a fine Irish linen cloth with a crocheted border of some Celtic design. In the center of the table stood a delicate, blue crystal vase with gold edges, which usually held a sprig of wildflowers. There was also an incense holder made of brass in which she burned the aromatic pellets of jasmine she bought at the five-and-dime. It filled the room with a heavy smoke that smelled, according to Donovan, like a farmer's ditch after it had been torched. But no one seemed to mind, though it was sometimes hard to tell what caused the clients' tears—the incense or their immediate problems.

While not being altogether unsuperstitious, Donovan still scoffed at the notion that Aunt Clare possessed any special gift, though he credited her with being a wonderful psychologist. Whether or not her specialty was better suited for a painted canvas tent and crystal ball, Aunt Clare's clients trusted in her magic. People claimed Aunt Clare had healed everything from rheumatism to wayward spouses. She easily solved June Grayson's problem with her unaffectionate cat by stuffing catnip in the batting of a quilt. It's still a mystery how one of her quilts cured Reverend Springwell's stuttering, but the congregation at the Calvary Baptist Church have not complained since.

After a short consultation that stirred the muddied scent of

wool, linen, cotton, other assorted fabrics and incense smoke, Aunt Clare always knew just what to do. "Now just you don't worry yourself," she would say, clutching their hands, as her nimble body sprang from the straight-backed chair, "I have just the solution."

"This is the one, my dear," said Aunt Clare to Gloria Hodge, a saddened, near-middle-aged woman who was childless. "This will do for you what science cannot." She placed a quilt on Gloria's lap.

"Oh my! Are you sure?" exclaimed Gloria. A wide-eyed, puzzled look spread across her face.

"Oh, absolutely, dear," said Aunt Clare in her sweet, squeaky voice. "Notice the pattern, how the circles are surrounded by interlocking lines." She moved her hand over the quilt. "This is designed specifically for childbearing, conception and other sexual things I won't elaborate upon."

"Isn't that too broad?" Gloria knew Aunt Clare's reputation for focusing on one specific problem.

"Good heavens, no," Aunt Clare blurted. "They're all interrelated, you know," she added, turning a little red.

"The color is…so…so unusual," said Gloria, toying with the edge of the quilt.

Aunt Clare's quilts were always unusual color combinations and patterns. Sometimes Donovan's younger sister, Sandy, would question her color choices.

"Are you sure you're not color blind, Aunt Clare?" Sandy would say.

"Heavens, no! Only men are color blind, dear," she would reply. "This is brown and that is blue," she would add and continue sewing her squares.

"Now don't you concern yourself with the colors," Aunt Clare reassured Gloria. "You have to start thinking of the lovely child you and John will have next spring." She held Gloria's hand, and explained the ways of her quilts. "Now just give it time," smiled Aunt Clare, escorting Gloria through the kitchen to the porch door. "Remember, the quilt must cover you and John every night for a fortnight. And don't forget the incense. It kindles the senses…and things."

Donovan was coming through the gate. "Just follow the instructions I gave you," Aunt Clare repeated as Gloria made her way down the path. Donovan smiled and greeted her as she drew near.

"Hello. I see you've been to see Aunt Clare."

"Yes. I sure hope she knows what she's doing."

"Oh, I'm sure of it," Donovan said and smiled politely.

"What's the occasion?" asked John Hodge with a glint in his eyes, as he entered the dimly lit bedroom and kicked off his shoes near the edge of the bed.

"I thought we would try again," Gloria said, slipping beneath the new cover on their bed.

In the dim light, the irregular angles in the bedroom of their Victorian house cast eerie shadows on the delicate flowered wallpaper. Above the large four-postered mahogany bed hung a Mary

Cassatt painting, *Mother and Child*. On the opposite wall was a Frida Kahlo print.

"Wonderful." John smiled at her as he unbuttoned his shirt, knowing how painful it was to discuss their situation. Looking quickly around the room, he asked, "Where is that smoke coming from?"

"It's incense. You like it?"

"I thought incense was supposed to smell nice," he said with a frown.

"It does, sort of," said Gloria, propping her head on her hand. "It's jasmine."

"I hope we don't die of smoke inhalation first," John chuckled, shaking his head as he reached down to pull back the cover on his side of the bed. Gloria watched him, smiling.

"This is new." John pulled up the corner of the quilt for a closer look. "Were the lights off in the store when you bought this?"

"It was given to me," replied Gloria. "Now are you going to get in here?"

John slid between the sheets. "That's even better. I'd hate to think that you actually bought something like that. Did you notice the colors?"

"Yes, love," answered Gloria. She turned off the nightstand lamp, to a resounding volley of sneezes.

"Incense," muttered John, as he caressed her tenderly.

———

Aunt Clare and Gloria stood on the back porch of the boarding house.

"That's wonderful, dear," beamed Aunt Clare, as Gloria gave her a tight hug.

"It's a miracle." A small tear ran down Gloria's cheek. Aunt Clare gently wiped it away with her scented cotton handkerchief. "And I owe it all to you, even though I had my doubts in the beginning."

"They all do, at first," Aunt Clare said, with a twinkle in her eyes. "But we've made a believer out of you, haven't we?"

"Yes," Gloria cooed, giving Aunt Clare another hug.

"And how does John feel?" The two stood holding onto each other's arms.

"He's so happy," replied Gloria in a bubbly voice. "But I never told him anything about the quilt."

"Just as well, dear," Aunt Clare giggled, infected with Gloria's joy. "He may not have understood."

"What's your secret? We tried for years—implantation, fertility drugs...but nothing worked."

"Modern science claims they can cure everything. But we know better, don't we?" replied Aunt Clare, tenderly squeezing Gloria's hand. "The secret's in the design and the color." A wide smile wrinkled Aunt Clare's sparkling eyes. "Among other things!"

"Well, however you do it, it's a miracle." Gloria stepped from the porch. Aunt Clare let the screen door release slowly from her delicate fingers, revealing her tiny silhouette behind the grey mesh.

The winds of late spring blew furiously the week Gloria Hodge gave birth. "It's a good thing, too," said Aunt Clare, sitting in the hospital waiting room holding John's hand as he nervously tapped his feet. "The wind is one big breath of life and that is what's going to happen tonight." Donovan sat in a wide, tangerine-colored chair across from them, thumbing through year-old magazines.

A young nurse called out John's name and told him to follow her. The trio silently made their way through the antiseptic corridors to reach the maternity viewing room.

"Oh my," exclaimed Aunt Clare. Her jaw dropped as she bent closer to the glass.

"Oh, dear God," sighed John.

The trio's faces were reflected in the safety glass. They stared at the blue and pink room full of bassinets, where two nurses were attending squirming, wailing bundles of new life. John stared blankly and kept repeating his initial response, over and over, until the viewing glass fogged with his breath.

"I hope this teaches you," Donovan quietly whispered into Aunt Clare's ear. "This time you've really done it."

"Oh, my," repeated Aunt Clare. She patted John on the shoulder and took Donovan's arm. "We'll be going now." She knew her words had not sunk in. They left him staring through the window, where a smile, beginning to bloom, radiated in the glass. He turned and rushed toward Gloria's room.

Word spread quickly about Gloria Hodge's miracle. In the weeks that followed, Aunt Clare was busy in her sewing room, helping one client after another. One day a line actually wound from her room across the kitchen and out the back door. Donovan and Sandy took turns serving coffee and finger sandwiches to the waiting guests. Tiny billows of incense spewed from beneath the closed door where Aunt Clare worked her magic. Donovan and Sandy shook their heads each time they saw someone leave the boarding house with an oddly colored quilt tucked in their arms. They looked at one another and laughed, visualizing the Hodges standing in their nursery the local Jaycees had built for them, looking down at the twisting, yawning, kicking life beneath Aunt Clare's quilt, which Gloria had cut and re-stitched into three smaller pieces that would, in time, reveal their own special magic.

Sisters of Interment

 They were known as the Four Winds, which had nothing to do with mythological proportion and everything to do with monopolizing the town's party lines. But Donovan referred to his Aunt Clare and her friends as the sisters of interment, since much of their conversations encompassed every known aspect of the lives of the recently deceased. Clare Magruder, Alice Young, Bess Dowd and Maggie Carrington were Allegory Falls's mavens of funerary fact and fiction. They knew everyone, and made it a point to attend every funeral.

"Gossip and commiserating about arthritis and flatulence is one thing, but constantly talking about the dead as if you were expecting to bump into them at the general store is another. It's morbid, don't you think?" said Donovan one afternoon as Aunt Clare hung up the phone, folded the newspaper, and set it neatly on her reading table.

"Nonsense, dear," replied Aunt Clare, leaning back in the old rocker near the front window of her boarding house. "It's just a way to rekindle old memories. You'll understand once you get to be our age."

One Wednesday in late summer, *The Allegory Falls Republican* published a death notice that stirred the depths of their collective memories. It read:

MYLES O. RANDOM
Myles Random, 84, died at his home in Lonestar.
Funeral services will be 2 p.m. Friday, August 12 at
Sunset Garden Funeral Home. Burial will follow at
Canyon View Cemetery.

Like clockwork, the phone service in Allegory Falls was disrupted at precisely 1:04 p.m. that hot, muggy day, when the four women began recounting their versions of the life and times of Myles Random, who, as history held, had briefly toyed with each of their affections.

"I had no idea Myles lived near us," bemoaned Maggie in her raspy voice.

"He didn't," Clare said sharply. "His body was shipped here to be buried next to his family."

"I remember that his family was from Texas," stated Bessie, hesitantly. "Yes, he was from Texas."

"No, no dear," replied Alice in a gentle, miniature voice. "They were from Chicago somewhere. Moved here in 1906."

"No," Clare said. "It was Colorado. 1905. It was my seventh birthday."

"I remember how dashingly handsome he was after the war…all his colored medals dangling from his uniform as he led the parade down Main Street. He was such a sight," sighed Maggie.

"You're breathing heavy, again," said Clare.

"He wasn't in the war and he most certainly never led a parade," Bessie exclaimed. "You're confusing him with Horace Pidge."

"Who's Pidge?" chirped Alice.

"Yes, Myles was a captain or lieutenant or something," Clare said. "He was on a roan horse with a flag, followed by eight others who went off to France. I'm sure of it."

"Who's Pidge?" Alice asked again.

"Forget Pidge, Alice. Myles moved away sometime after the war," Maggie answered quickly. "We dated once before he left for France. I remember how tall he was and how he combed his rich, black hair to the side and…"

"Myles was not tall and he never parted his hair," said Bessie, taking a deep breath. "He was average size with auburn hair and rascally dimples, but not all *that* handsome." But the very recollection of Myles Random, nonetheless took her breath away.

"You're just jealous because I got to play Ophelia to Myles's Hamlet that summer at the Moxie theater. He had a strong face and could have been another Douglas Fairbanks, I say," insisted Clare.

"He was more suited for Puck, if you ask me," grumbled Bess.

"Well, I think you're all muddle-headed today," Alice boldly added. "Myles had puffy jowls, squatty legs, a red face and hair to match. You are all mistaking him for someone else. Douglas Fairbanks—phooey."

"No we are not, Alice!" the others replied in unison.

"It's Pidge you're describing, not Myles," said Bess.

"I wonder why Myles ever left Allegory Falls?" Maggie said.

"He was much too talented to waste his life away here. A war hero, college graduate and engineer. Myles was destined to leave," Bessie sadly intoned. "The good ones always slip away."

"Of course, he had to leave! Clare's father made sure of that. He had no choice," replied Alice, twisting a little thorn.

"That wasn't the reason and you know it!" snapped Clare. "He left Allegory Falls for a job in South America—Bolivia, I think— building electric dams."

Maggie didn't let Clare change the subject. "I think Alice is right about your father, Clare."

"Just never you mind," said Clare. "You're all dizzy today."

"You know, Clare, what with you fawning over him all the time, and in public, no less, what were people to think?" stated Bessie. "I don't blame your father for chasing him off. Who knows what would have happened had he not."

"And you should talk, Bessie," piped Alice. "I still remember the rumor about you and Myles after you two were caught in a moment of, say, awkwardness in the hayloft after the Halloween dance."

"I most definitely never fawned," said Clare.

"It wasn't the hayloft," Bessie asserted. "It was the wood-shed."

"That's right! It was Maggie in the hayloft," Clare said.

"That wasn't Myles, and you know it," said Maggie. "Besides, none of us have any more secrets, and if we did, we've probably forgotten them."

"One can never be sure," chuckled Clare. Her mind drifted to the past as the others continued resurrecting Myles O. Random. Clare was sure. Sure, at least, of the many details she would never reveal to her friends, as dear as they were to her.

——

"You don't have any plans for Saturday night, do you, Myles?" asked Clare, as she and her friends sat outside Smith's Drugstore eating ice cream sundaes.

"Clare!" said two of her friends.

Clare's sparkling blue eyes and dimpled pink cheeks raged with a spirited, flirtatious glow. "I was only asking," she replied, smiling at Myles.

"I was thinking of going to the dance with Horace and a few other friends," answered Myles.

"Why not take me instead?" Clare asked. "I'd be a lot more fun than Horace and the boys."

Maggie, Bess and Alice's jaws dropped.

"Why don't we just all go together," piped Bess. Alice and Maggie nodded their heads in agreement.

"We always do that," complained Clare. "I'd rather have Myles take me this time."

That silly jealousy had kept the four friends apart the summer of 1920, as Myles and Clare spent more and more time together.

——

"Do you remember the time we all went swimming together after the war?" Alice asked.

"Swimming?" replied Clare, suddenly awakened from her daydream.

"Oh, yes, the swimming party," cooed Maggie. "Myles was there."

"Oh, that," replied Clare. "Myles was with me, if you remember."

"We know, Clare," snipped Bessie. "What an embarrassment you were to us."

"Me?" spewed Clare. "And what about you? Not just you, Bessie, but all of you? You all are still mad at me for inviting Myles to that summer dance, aren't you?" she added.

"At the time…and maybe just a little bit now. I don't know, but I do know that proper young ladies shouldn't act the way you did then. It was highly improper," said Bessie.

"I don't remember any dance," said Alice.

"Never mind, dear. Let's get back to the swimming party and how Clare brazenly treated us all," said Maggie. "I want to know why you did what you did."

"We don't need to discuss that," snapped Clare, wanting to evade the details of that long-ago afternoon.

"I still don't know what possessed you to do that," Alice said, obviously still embarrassed fifty-some years later. "What were you thinking?"

"Yes, Clare, what were you trying to prove?" asked Maggie.

"As if you all didn't know," quipped Clare, "what with your fawning over Myles the entire day. Now that was fawning. I couldn't spend a minute alone with him without one of you interrupting in some fashion. So I did what I did. And it worked! You all had dates, but you just couldn't leave Myles alone. Maggie fussing over him during lunch like he was a helpless child. And Bess—did you once say anything to your date? It was always Myles this and Myles that. Alice, you were the best of the three, but you couldn't hide those looks you were flashing Myles all through lunch. And you call me an embarrassment?" Clare was nearly out of breath. "How many war stories about Paris can one hear? And to think none of you ever bothered asking Horace or Charles or Billy how they felt or what..." The pique arose in her as it had on that day so many years ago. The crackle of silence on the party line drew her back to those memories with Myles.

———

Clare had become so frustrated with the others' behavior that day that she resorted to an impetuous measure. She abruptly stood up and walked to the edge of the lake. Stripping off her bathing suit, she faced the others, quickly thumbed her nose, and dove into the cold water of the mountain lake.

Charles, who was with Alice, developed a sudden paroxysm while sipping his tea. Clare's girlfriends hurriedly tried to cover the eyes of their dates. Bessie tripped over Charles trying to shield Pidge and accidently poked Billy in the eye with her teaspoon. Myles let loose a nervous laugh. Those French postcards he had collected did not begin to compare to Clare's beauty as she bounded out of the water when she saw the chaos on the shore. Grabbing her swimming suit, she walked up to the others without any regard for appearance, and asked Myles to take her home. She then proceeded to the car and sat there naked, beaded with shimmering droplets of water while the others mumbled and scurried off to their cars.

———

Clare remained miles away on that mid-August afternoon as the others continued to reminisce about Myles.

Myles and Clare had stopped and walked along a mountain meadow dwarfed by an overhanging steel-blue canyon wall that reflected in the clear water of the lake. They sat among the wildflowers, marveling at the beauty before them. Summer was always a time of magic and unsuspected drama in Allegory Falls. They lay back, their bodies cushioned by the thick layers of bunch grasses and wildflowers, while the scent of pine and fir pirouetted on the delicate breeze that swept off the mountain.

"You really embarrassed your friends," said Myles, as he tenderly ran his fingers along Clare's face.

"They had it coming," said Clare.

"Are you jealous?" Myles asked.

"I thought I was losing you," she replied. "Besides, they'll get over it in time."

"You'll never lose me." Myles watched Clare blink her eyes over and over. "What are you doing?"

"Looking at the sunlight. If you let the light bathe your eyes while you blink over and over, it's like a kaleidoscope. Try it."

Their faces were afire with a halo of bright colors that danced across the soft contours of their skin.

"You're right," said Myles. "It's like looking into the eyes of heaven."

Clare turned to Myles with a sprig of wildflowers between her fingers. "Were you serious when you said that I'd never lose you?"

"Yes." Myles took the flowers. "We will never lose each other."

Clare and Myles walked across the meadow slowly and silently, as shades of indigo washed the sky, to an old homesteader's cabin that Clare's father had converted to a summer house.

"Is anything the matter, Clare?" asked Bessie. "You haven't said a word these past few minutes, dear. Did we upset you?"

"No, I'm quite fine," said Clare, recovering from her daydreams.

"What's past is past," said Maggie, sighing heavily. "We were just chasing a youthful dream. Why, until today, I hadn't thought about Myles...well, in ages."

"Me either," replied Alice and Bess in unison.

"Just a piece of the quilt," Clare said, smiling. "And there are so many pieces to a quilt." She pulled a worn photograph from the curved drawer of her reading table. It was a picture of Myles and her before he left Allegory Falls. She leaned it against the lamp as Alice's voice came through the receiver.

"So what time shall we meet on Friday? One-thirty?"

"One-thirty should do just fine," answered Bessie.

The four friends entered the funeral parlor at 1:30 p.m. Two by two they walked up the aisle, across a narrow and worn carpet runner, and took seats in the front row. They and Mr. Nussbaum, the portly, asthmatic undertaker, were the only ones in attendance. Minutes passed. Then a half-hour. No one else came. Horace Pidge and the others had long since passed on.

The ladies stared at the highly polished cherry casket, draped by a large bouquet of wildflowers tied with a red ribbon. The vacuumous silence was finally broken when the two-o'clock bells pealed from St. Luke's. Nussbaum slowly paced to the casket and opened it for viewing. The old women sat, like crows on a fence line, watching Nussbaum's every move until he finally retreated into the recesses of the parlor behind the heavy, gold draperies.

The four ladies arose in unison and approached the coffin, as they had done on many such occasions at Sunset Garden Funeral Home. Myles Random, powdered, pale blue cold, with rouged cheeks, arms folded to his chest, lay before them. One by one, they spoke reverently, with little animation in their voices, as they looked upon the corpse bedded on white, billowy satin.

"I don't remember him being so...short," said one.

"I don't remember him being so...so...unattractive," said another, her face contorted.

The four stood over Myles in a moment of silence. Clare longed to reach out and touch him—a brush across his brow, a kiss on his cheek, remembering the words he had spoken those many years ago. As the light pierced the stained glass and broke into a kaleidoscope of colors, Clare knew that Myles had never left her.

"I don't know why he's not in his uniform," whispered Maggie.

"There's no way he could fit into that uniform unless he lost near forty pounds," said Bessie.

"I wonder who provided the flowers?" said Alice.

"Not very dignified for a funeral if you ask me," said Bessie, "but for wild weeds, they are spectacular."

"Yes, they are quite lovely," said Maggie.

A big smile squirmed across Clare's face.

The four turned toward the parlor door. Clare stopped at the door long enough to glance back a final time just as Nussbaum closed the casket.

"Yes, I think he would have liked the wildflowers very much," she said softly.

désert

mushrooms

 "Are you just going to sit there and stare off into space all day," hollered Aunt Clare to Donovan from the kitchen door, "or are you going to finish your chores?"

"Yes, ma'am, coming," said Donovan, perched precariously on the moss-covered shingled roof with a safety rope tied to the ornate cupola. He had just finished cleaning a year's worth of pigeon residue from the three chimneys and two cupolas.

"I want you to take this ointment over to the Zaveta place," Aunt Clare said when Donovan stepped off the ladder. "He's expecting you right away."

"Why do I have to do it?" asked Donovan, untying the rope from his waist. "That place gives me the creeps."

Donovan had never seen Anthony Zaveta, but he had heard stories from those who supposedly had who said he looked like a character from the *Twilight Zone*. Aunt Clare said it was all made up, though she had never seen Zaveta clearly either.

"Now, Donovan, Anthony is a pleasant man—a little lonely, but easy to talk to once you get to know him. It won't hurt you to do it just this once. I have a funeral to attend at 2:00 p.m. and your sister is cleaning rooms. I promised I would get this to him soon."

"Alright," Donovan replied reluctantly. "You know, your quilts are one thing, but giving people homemade medicine is another. It's going to get you in trouble someday."

"Nonsense, dear. It's just some harmless ingredients. Why, I've used it on you for years." She chuckled and went back inside. Donovan shook his head, looking at the small, opaque jar Aunt Clare had left on the patio table.

Anthony Zaveta's house was easily visible from the roof of Aunt Clare's boarding house. The depression-era dwelling sat on twelve lamentable acres baking in the midsummer sun. Its loose siding and broken shutters moaned with each gust of wind. Flakes of multicolored lead paint, from years of painting, lay at the foot of the stone foundation like a coral snake that had shed its skin. Beyond the small screened porch stood a few wiry carcasses of apple trees that had long been forgotten.

Donovan made his way quietly up the porch, hoping to set the jar by the door, knock and quickly vanish. But fearing Aunt Clare's wrath, he hesitantly tapped on Zaveta's door.

"It's unlocked," rang out a craggy voice.

Donovan opened the door. The intense light of the summer's day infused the blackness of the room as he nervously stood in the doorway.

"Mr. Zaveta, sir?"

"Get in here and shut that damn door," bellowed Zaveta. Donovan felt the living room shudder when he quickly closed the door.

The room was pitch black and smelled like a root cellar. Donovan blinked his eyes slowly, trying to see. Zaveta was just a vague shape in a big armchair. "My aunt wanted me to bring this medicine to you," he stammered.

"Took you long enough. I guess you didn't take your aunt seriously. When she said I needed it right away she meant it," Zaveta grumbled. His rattling sigh sounded like marbles in a tobacco tin.

Donovan caught his foot on the corner of the couch as he made his way toward the dark specter in the corner.

"Just set it on the table next to me," Zaveta said.

Unaccustomed to the darkness, Donovan fumbled for the table's edge. The jar hit the wooden floor.

"I've got it," he said, dropping to his knees and groping about the floor, where forgotten orts stuck to his hands.

"Light bothers me," Zaveta explained. The springs in his chair creaked as he shifted his weight. "Now sit down. I get tired look-ing up."

"I really should be going," said Donovan.

"Your aunt always sits with me awhile. I don't get many visitors."

"I guess I could stay a minute then," Donovan felt for the couch.

"It's right there, behind you," said Zaveta.

"Oh, yes." Donovan felt swallowed up by the soft, plush couch.

"Clare makes the best medicine!" Zaveta said fervently. "I don't know what I'd do without her."

"She's very handy."

"Handy? Why, she's a genius!" Donovan heard the lid of the jar turning. "Fall isn't far off," Zaveta said. "It's the summer I can't stand—too hot and too bright." The outline of his hands moved across his face.

"Ever thought of moving to a cooler climate?" asked Donovan.

"Plenty of times, but there isn't much sense in that at my age."

He rubbed more of the creamy ointment over his face. Then he paused, and began to tell Donovan a story. As bartender at Haig's, Donovan was used to people telling him their life stories, but he wasn't prepared for the one Zaveta told.

"I had this girlfriend once, her name was Ramona," Zaveta began. "Only one I ever had. I used to spend summers with my uncle—his wife had Ramona from a previous marriage. She was about the same age as me—couple of months younger, I think," he added, wheezing. "They lived on a ranch outside Las Vegas, up near Indian Springs. I helped with the chores, for which my uncle would buy me new clothes for school and give me a dollar or two. My folks were dirt poor and just getting started with the orchard business. Ramona and I didn't like each other in the beginning, but the summer we turned seventeen we began paying a lot of attention to one another. Funny how nature times everything out just right." Zaveta coughed.

"You all right?" asked Donovan, leaning forward on the couch.

"I'm all right," said Zaveta. "Just relax, it's the heat is all. As I was saying, we hit it off really well that summer. Weren't out of each other's sight for more than a minute. It was sweet."

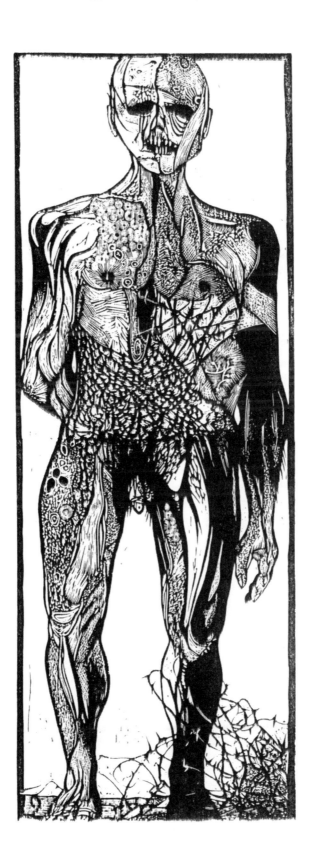

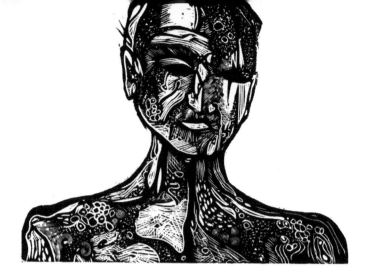

"She must have been very special."

"She was. And very beautiful…and that's what I regret the most." His voice saddened.

"I don't understand," replied Donovan.

"I don't think I ever told her how beautiful she was."

"You must have," began Donovan, suddenly feeling the need to comfort him. "At least, if not in words, then in some other way."

"I don't think so."

"Couldn't you tell her now?" Donovan asked gingerly.

"She's been gone for a lot of years now."

"I'm sorry. Can I ask what happened?"

"That's very kind of you," Zaveta said. "What did we know as kids? One Saturday night, on a back road of their enormous ranch, we drove the old Jeep near the crest of a ridge. There was straw, some blankets and a saddle in the back—I remember that because the straw made me itch all over. I broke out in hives later that night and Ramona's mother had to rub a poultice all over me." Zaveta sighed as he relived his youth. The room was silent except for his heavy, labored breathing.

"Ramona said she had a surprise for me," he continued. "She told me to watch the sky. I figured it was one of those meteor showers or a star or something. She liked that sort of thing. We talked and kissed and looked up at the stars every now and then.

Anyway, her surprise finally showed up." Zaveta rose from his chair suddenly. Donovan, his eyes adjusted to the darkness, watched him hobble out of the room and heard the running of water and the tinkling of ice against glass in the kitchen.

"Here," said Zaveta, putting a glass in front of Donovan's face. "It's right in front of you."

"You can see everything in this darkness?" asked Donovan, staring into the blackness while Zaveta reseated himself in the chair.

"Perfectly. My eyes have accustomed themselves to the intense darkness after all these years."

"Then you never go out?"

"Not if I can help it, and then only at night. My appearance frightens people…now where was I?"

"The surprise," said Donovan.

"Oh yes, the surprise!" Zaveta sighed. "We lay there, in the back of that Jeep, against that saddle for what seemed like hours. The times you miss the most are the ones you want to last for eternity…but they don't." Zaveta paused to take a sip of water and suck on a piece of ice, which clicked against his teeth.

"We were fooling around real serious, and then her surprise came off in the distance on the desert floor. The night sky erupted with the fire and light of a hundred suns. It sucked all the coolness out of the night air. I remember that part real good. We sat there in awe—it looked like a huge desert mushroom on fire. We just sat there without saying a word until the sky went black again. I remember how the warm pelting wind rushed against our bodies and engulfed us as we lay back on the blanket."

Donovan heard the mixture of wonderment and sadness in Zaveta's tired voice. "That's…that's…" he stuttered.

"Pretty amazing. I thought so, too, once," said Zaveta, quietly.

"Then what happened?" asked Donovan, quelling his shock.

"I returned here for school that fall, but I saw her again the next summer, after we both graduated. It was a wonderful summer— even grander than the previous one. We watched another desert mushroom burn one night, but then my mother got sick and I had to come home. Ramona and I made plans to get married, but…" Zaveta paused and put his empty glass on the reading table next to him.

"Why didn't you?" Donovan asked.

"I never saw her again after that summer." Zaveta wheezed and cleared his throat. "She got bone cancer and went real fast. I tried to make it back to her, but I was too late—too late to tell her how beautiful she was to me. So I came home to be with my mother. My dad passed on shortly after, and I just let things go. Never felt too good myself—expect I've got the cancer, too, only it's taking a lot longer to kill me. We didn't know any better in those days."

"I don't know what to say." Donovan sighed. "I wish I could do…"

"That's all right," answered Zaveta, his words muffled as he rubbed more of Aunt Clare's ointment on his lips. "It was a long time ago. Kinda funny how, when you want things to pass quickly, they seem to end up lasting forever—just like this damned, infernal summer. Have you ever had a girl?"

"Not seriously like you."

"Well, if you do, don't forget to tell her how beautiful she is," he said.

Donovan's chest heaved with sorrow. They sat in the darkness quietly telling each other stories as the afternoon slipped away.

"Sorry I yelled at you when you first came in," Zaveta said. "I get ornery once in a while, but I don't mean nothing by it. I appreciate you bringing your aunt's medicine. Hope you can come back again—I liked talking with you."

Donovan stood up. "I enjoyed it, too. And next time, I won't be late." Donovan made his way out the door, where the setting sun fanned a brilliant red-orange swath across the horizon. For a moment, he thought he could see Ramona's beautiful face in a billowing, distant cloud. But only for a moment.

JACKSON
POLLOCK'S COW

 The frozen air from an early November blizzard swirled around Donovan as he drove along a lonely stretch of road toward Tom Breechman's ranch, nestled in the breaks west of Allegory Falls. The memories of a long summer could not dispel the gnawing chill. Drifts of snow hooded the tops of fenceposts and the sagging strands of barbed wire sparkled like strings of pearls.

Breechman was coming down his porch steps when Donovan coasted into the driveway and silenced the sputtering engine of his truck. Tom was a squatty man with a craggy face that rarely changed expression. A sweat-stained John Deere cap was pushed back on his forehead, and sprigs of graying hair jutted at odd angles across his brow. Breechman's eyes were dark and brooding and marshaled themselves to every move that Donovan made.

Breechman tugged at the sleeves of his yellow slicker to loosen a balled-up clot of denim shirt and closed the slicker over his 12-pack paunch. His voice sawed through the stiff air.

"Szylokowski said you'd be here at noon. You're late." He paused and pulled gloves from his pockets while Donovan gathered his equipment from the seat of the truck. "Follow me and try not to get lost—I've wasted enough time waiting for you already." He stomped off up the road.

Tom and his blue-heeler dog pushed through the snow toward the bench land he used as winter pasture. Donovan followed behind as they moved beyond the outlying corrals and shed blanketed with a foot of fresh snow. For nearly an hour, the threesome trudged through timber and underbrush until they finally reached a small clearing at the crest of a ridge. Donovan had barely left the final thicket when Tom grabbed him by his coat sleeve and pulled him to a rounded heap covered by thick snow. "There it is!"

Donovan brushed snow from his collar and silently cursed Szylokowski for having sent him on this job.

"See what?" he asked.

"It's right in front of you!" Breechman bellowed. "The heap." He bent down and brushed off the fresh carpet of snow to reveal what was left of one of his prized Angus cows. His dog pawed and licked the carcass until Breechman gave it a whack with a wet leather glove. Both Tom and the dog seemed to be yelping in excitement until a deep, volcanic laugh welled up inside Donovan.

"What in the hell are you laughing at?" puffed Tom, still clearing the remains of the cow.

"This! Who cares about a frozen cow?"

"Well, funny man, you won't be laughing when I show you the evidence. There it is!" Tom rose to his feet and pointed.

Mutilated cows were nothing new—they had appeared in many places across the West—but this was Allegory Falls's first reported case and Stan Szylokowski, managing editor of the *Allegory Falls Republican*, wanted to keep pace with the newspapers whose sensationalized stories blared from the front pages. As the newspaper's part-time photographer, Donovan tried to dissuade Szylokowski, but cows in any shape, color or form were popular news items in Allegory Falls. In fact, stories on cattle ranked ahead of religion, politics and sex scandals. So there Donovan stood, shivering in the fading afternoon light, with his camera in hand, before a dead, mangled, Red Angus cow.

"OK, this will work," he said, changing positions and depressing the shutter button. "Good. Just one more and we'll be out of here." He sounded like he was photographing a super model, not a mutilated cow, when Breechman shouted at him.

"No, no, no! You tyro! Get closer! It ain't gonna bite!"

Cold, wet but too tired to argue, Donovan decided to pacify the old codger. He got down on his knees and snapped one close-up after another of the frozen blood, mangled flesh and charred, hairy remains.

"That's better. Now you look like you know what you are doing with that thing," said Breechman. "This will show them that aliens were here." A frozen, toothy smile stretched across his face and he paced back and forth behind Donovan, whose camera hissed and whined.

"Aliens?" Donovan glanced over his shoulder dubiously at

Breechman.

"Yeah, what'd you think—some weirdo cult did this in the middle of a blizzard? You nuts?"

"Well, I'm not sure these pictures will work," Donovan said, rising to his feet and dusting off the snow frozen to his jeans.

"Why not? Szylokowski says you're a genius with a camera."

"Black-and-white close-ups never reproduce well in print—too muddied. Besides, people won't recognize what they are looking at," explained Donovan. "This could end up looking like...like a Jackson Pollock drip painting."

"And what's wrong with Jackson Pollock?" Tom scowled and perched his hands on what waistline he had left.

Donovan had covered many stories for Stan Szylokowski and not once had the subject of Jackson Pollock come up. Allegory Falls was not a hotbed of fine art and culture. Donovan remembered that it had taken ten years for *Easy Rider* to make it to the Moxie theater and by then everyone was caught up in the *Star Wars* phenomenon.

Breechman looked at him impatiently. "We're not all as unsophisticated as you might think. I just so happen to subscribe to a great many periodicals, including some of them artsy ones."

"I didn't mean to..." Donovan was speechless.

"I collect a lot of those pictures. Cut them out and paste them to the walls and ceiling of my bedroom. I like laying back and looking at them before I go to sleep—helps me relax," said Tom, pleased with himself and his handiwork. "It's like my own Sistine Chapel."

"I had no idea," said Donovan, somewhat embarrassed. "I didn't mean to be so presumptuous."

"Yeah, yeah, whatever. Those magazines—that's where I learned about Pollock. He doesn't inspire me though—I prefer realism and nudes. Especially nudes." He added in a cocky voice, "But I know of Pollock."

"Then you understand that a close-up will look more like one of his paintings than a dead cow," Donovan said, feeling more confident.

"*Mutilated* cow!" shouted Tom, insisting on the seriousness of the situation.

"Sorry," said Donovan, closing his camera case.

"You know, Pollock lived in the country, too. Probably got his ideas in the first place from looking at mutilated cows...or drinking." Tom stopped abruptly. "But those pictures don't lie," he mumbled. He and the dog started ahead of Donovan back down the bench land.

It was late afternoon when they arrived wearily back at Tom's house. "Don't you worry none," said Breechman. "If those pictures look anything like Jackson Pollock's art, then our work will be done. People will be convinced that other powers are at work here, for that ain't natural or real what happened to that cow."

And with that, Breechman bounded up the stoop of his porch, which groaned with every step, and held the door open until his dog finally made up its mind to go inside.

"You get them?" asked Szylokowski, when Donovan came through the employees' entrance of the pressroom.

"Yeah, and I should charge you twice what I normally do for this job!" snapped Donovan, taking the film from his camera.

"It couldn't have been that bad," said Stan, putting down some copy. "I interviewed Tom over the phone yesterday and he seemed alright to me."

"Maybe you should have taken the photos, then," said Donovan, slapping the roll of film in his hand.

"What's this?"

"Jackson Pollock's Cow," Donovan said in disgust.

"What?"

"Evidence from the Breechman place." Donovan left the building, with Szylokowski on his heels.

"Hey! Aren't you going to develop it and pull a proof we can use?"

"No, Stan," Donovan replied, opening the door of his truck and sliding onto the cold, brittle seat. "You do it. You're the one who wanted to do the story in the first place, remember?"

"See if I hire you anymore!" yelled Stan, as Donovan raced the engine.

"Who else are you going to get, huh, Stanley?" Donovan disappeared down the back alley in a cloud of blue exhaust.

The following morning, Donovan sat in the kitchen, wrapped in one of his aunt's quilts, still cold from his experience at the

Breechman ranch. He grabbed the morning paper, neatly folded on the kitchen table, and drew his chair nearer the wood cook stove, whose belly was roaring. He opened the paper to see what Stan had chosen for the headline, and when he unfurled it with a snap, he could not believe what he saw.

Szylokowski had done it. "ALIENS MUTILATE COW" the banner read, above a small photo of Tom and his dog that Donovan had inadvertently snapped, and a nearly half-page photo that looked, just as he had imagined, like a detail from Pollock's painting, *Shimmering Substance*.

The article and photos swallowed most of the front page, except for a short piece on how Craving's Sporting Goods had completely sold out of ammunition, rifles and duck blinds. There was also a one-paragraph snippet about two lost, out-of-state hunters who had miraculously survived the recent three-day blizzard by living off the land.

Donovan laid the paper aside and huddled over the radiating cast iron. He closed his eyes and visualized Tom lying on his bed, staring at the ceiling with its cutouts of famous and not-so-famous works of art, which now undoubtedly included something that only looked as if it had been painted by Jackson Pollock.

 Donovan Magruder and John McGunnigan were sitting at the Ranch Cafe's crusty, worn orange lunch counter beneath the painful turning of the ceiling fan one bitterly cold day when Edward John Patrick Kelly walked through the door and sat at a corner table by the steamed window. Kelly was a small-town hero whose armor was tarnished and pitted like the cafe's bricked facade. The old pugilist stared forlornly out the window, wiping the brittle pane where paper-thin sheets of ice slid down the glass and collected in tiny pools on the windowsill.

Donovan quietly watched Kelly. "Have you ever wondered if there's something more to Kelly's life than the portrait he paints?" he asked McGunnigan.

It was true that Kelly told and retold stories about his days in the boxing ring in exchange for drinks at the Workman's Bar. He was always surrounded by a few regulars who paid reverence and offered their empathy. Small-town athletes have a way of recycling the past, and like a medieval court, are never without an audience paying tribute.

A frown creased McGunnigan's face as he wiped bits of potato cakes from his mouth. "Kelly? No. What you see is what you get."

Donovan ignored the comment. He remembered his own childhood when he, McGunnigan and Itty McNeal took boxing lessons at the VFW, where Kelly had gotten his start decades before. "The posters old Pops Flannery put up said something about the man—he was always trying to get us to imitate Kelly. There was more to it than boxing lessons."

"As a matter of fact, yes," replied McGunnigan. "Pops was try- ing to say the opposite—Kelly boxed, made a reputation for him- self, and lost the big one. Life. He now relives a few blurry years of his past over and over, with the help of Jack Daniels. That's what Pops was trying to teach you."

"You're wrong. He has to be more than—" began Donovan.

"The poster child for bag people," interjected McGunnigan.

"That's too easy. No one's life is that simple," replied Donovan, turning on his stool.

"Suit yourself," replied McGunnigan. "He's right there. Find out for yourself."

"You coming along?" asked Donovan.

"I've heard my share," replied McGunnigan. He put three dol- lars on the counter and left the cafe. A cold rush of air gripped Donovan as he slowly walked toward Kelly.

Kelly was warming his neglected, aging body over a bowl of the cafe's watery cream of wheat. His face, desperately in need of a shave, was a geometric puzzle of unnatural angles, pockmarked, dry and spongy as boiled pigskin. His scarred eyes were reduced to thin slits that concealed dull, bloodshot eyes. He sniffed the steam from his cereal through the broken cartilage of his flattened nose. Neglect had rotted his teeth until his smile looked like the heavily pounded piano keyboard that sat in the corner of the Workman's Bar.

Donovan had seen the Kid earlier that winter in the Work- man's, a small, dimly lit saloon, where a small crowd of regulars gathered around a wobbly circular table to listen to the Kid's stories of his pugilistic conquests. After a few drinks turned his foggy memory to an impenetrable maze, Kelly would embellish his stories with outrageous details to the delight of his listeners.

"Tell us about Bulldog McCafferty again," someone had said, as Donovan pushed his way through the small throng close to the table.

"Bulldog!" snorted the Kid. "More like a damn cur. One punch. One punch was all it took." Everyone laughed along with the Kid except Donovan, who sensed a shallowness in Kelly's raspy voice. The sweetened plots he wove rotted the truth of the matter, but no one seemed to mind Kelly's inconsistent fabrications.

"Get me another and I'll tell you about the Sicilian Hammer— he wasn't much of a boxer either," laughed Kelly, as someone handed him a drink. "Don't get me wrong, he was a mean sono-fabitch, but like I said, no boxer. He liked coming in straight on and staying close. He got his nickname from his style. He had unusually large arms for a lightweight and he'd get close and bring them up and try to hit you on top of the head."

"So did he tag you good, Kid?" someone asked.

"Once. You know I'm about two inches shorter now, don't you?" Kelly chuckled again. "He went to the well once too often, and I caught him with an uppercut in the third round."

"What about Battista?" asked Donovan. The onlookers fell silent and stared at him. Kelly never discussed that fight. It was his last, one that had cost him the North American championship and the chance to fight for the world championship.

"What about him!" Kelly slammed his empty glass against the table. "Who said that?" he added, looking at everyone.

One of the patrons hurried another drink to the Kid. Donovan insinuated himself into the crowd as Kelly refreshed himself and continued pounding out his innocuous stories.

———

"You're Kid Kelly." Donovan sat down across from Kelly. "I heard a couple of your stories at the Workman's Bar weeks past."

"Yeah, what of it?" challenged the Kid in his gruff, low voice, without looking up to see who had disturbed him during the only meal he could afford.

"You're a local legend, and I was wondering if…" Donovan grinned nervously.

"Get lost," snapped the Kid, between slurps of cereal. "I'm eating."

"You were one of the greats," said Donovan. Kelly's eyes brightened like the moon shining in brown, muddy pools. For an instant, Donovan saw the fierce, raw-edged self-assuredness of the Kid he had seen in all those posters.

"What do you know?" grumbled Kelly. "You ever box?"

"Took lessons from Pops Flannagan, like you," replied Donovan.

"Any good?"

"No. Never liked being hit."

"Probably for the best. Otherwise you might be sitting where I am. Still box?"

"No."

"So what do you do?" asked Kelly.

"Odds and ends, right now, but I want to be a writer someday," answered Donovan.

"Newspaper writer?"

"No. Fiction. Stories about people."

Kelly thought for a moment. "Well, I don't have a story for you, if that's why you're here. But you made a better choice for your life than I did."

"Then you've regretted your choices?" Donovan looked at Kelly's hands, twisted and gnarled like whorls of dried grapevines. Once they were fast, lethal with power; now they shook with the weight of his spoon.

Kelly gave Donovan a good looking over, like he was sizing up an opponent. "You always been this tenacious?"

"I suppose. Some people say I ask too many questions," replied Donovan.

"Yeah, well, that's okay. Most don't ask enough of them. Well, I'll tell you a story," began Kelly. "I was almost twenty-eight when I fought Battista for the regional championship in Las Vegas. You've probably seen those posters Pops put up?" Kelly paused and sprinkled more sugar in his bowl. "They called him the Mad

Matador. He was from Mexico somewhere. Latinos like macho names—I do too, but being Irish, I was stuck with 'the Kid.' Pop pinned that one on me. Said Irish boxers are supposed to be called Kid."

"What did you want to be called?" asked Donovan, resting his elbows on the table.

"If I had a choice? Killer, maybe," Kelly said wistfully.

A few posters of the Battista fight still remained around town, covered with graffiti.

"You always wanted to be a fighter, though?"

"Never knew anything else. After my mother passed away, I hung out at the VFW. My father drank and was mean. My brothers were a lot older, so I boxed. I got real good, pretty quick. Pops told my father I could be a pro, so I was pushed harder by the two of them. I started out making five bucks a fight, beating some

kid senseless." A look of sadness washed over Kelly as if he pitied their weakness. The old boxer took a deep breath and exhaled it slowly. "Why aren't you writing this down?"

Donovan fumbled beneath his coat for a pen. He grabbed a few napkins from the sticky holder and scribbled a line or two.

"That's better. If you're gonna write this, you got to get it right."

Donovan nodded and continued to write as Kelly spoke. He knew now that McGunnigan and all the rest were wrong about the Kid. There was something more to his story.

"My father became my manager— neither Pops or me had much say in the matter. We spent most of the year on the road, in small towns like this one. My reputation grew as fast as my challengers fell. Another town, another smokey ring, another fight. There was always another."

"What was it like?"

"Hard," Kelly answered. "I remember the fights, sure, but I also remember how my father would spend most of the time before the fights in the bars. Sometimes he would bet the local tough guy I could take him."

"And did you?"

"Didn't have much choice. Sometimes I'd go into the ring looking worse than the guy who would be leaving it. We were making the Dust Bowl circuit through Oklahoma and Texas. Somewhere in Texas—Amarillo, I think—my father came to me and told me to take a dive. I was young and mad and didn't understand. The more I asked why, the madder he got. I didn't find out until later that he was gambling more and drinking heavier, and owed a couple of promoters a lot of money." Kelly paused and rubbed his hands across his face.

Donovan stared at the napkin, where his ink was bleeding through the paper.

"I told him I couldn't do it," moaned Kelly. "Later, I was in the back room, getting dressed for the fight, when my father came up behind me real quiet like. I never heard him through the noise of the ongoing fight." Kelly sighed and looked into Donovan's eyes. "The sonofabitch hit me across the ribs with a lead pipe so hard I could barely breathe. It was on my right side, too. It took everything I had just to pull on my trunks."

Kelly stared out the window as Donovan fought with his emotions.

"Then you had to take the dive? You couldn't fight with that kind of injury," said Donovan.

"I could too," said Kelly proudly. "My father thought for sure I'd go down, but I showed that bastard. I never thought I'd get past the first round, so I charged him, like the Sicilian Hammer used to do, using my left, and made quick work of the matter. I'd never take a dive for money."

"What about your father?"

"Last time I saw him alive." Kelly hung his head, his voice quivering. "They found him later in the alley. I didn't know, just didn't know, how deep he was into all that gambling business."

The two sat quietly as the waitress poured them coffee.

"My father had signed me over to them before they killed him. Things changed real fast after that. They treated me all right—better than what my father had."

"How could you keep fighting for the people who killed your father?"

"How could I not?" answered Kelly, gruffly. "I wasn't about to end up like my father, so I just kept fighting." He sipped his coffee. "I was young, used to being kicked around, and when they started flashing money around and paying fancy hookers to spend time with me, it was like they were making amends, somehow. I don't know…I don't think about it much."

Kelly searched for something more to say, but he was no philosopher.

"I was nothing special," he said slowly, a blank expression etched on his face.

"Then they groomed you for better fights?" asked Donovan.

"Better?"

"Bigger names, purses, you know."

"Oh, sure. They were in it for the money, as much as I was in it for the glory. Then came the Battista match."

"Could have been champ…maybe of the world," said Kelly. "I was sitting in the dressing room. It was the fanciest I'd ever been in, but it smelled like all the rest. They came to me like they came to my father."

"They wanted you to…" began Donovan.

"Yeah. They had bet a fortune on Battista. Said they'd kill me like they did my father," snapped the Kid. "It was the lowest point in my life." Kelly sat trancelike until the clunking of the heater awakened him.

He spelled out the details, round by round, of the match with

Battista. "They led me down the aisle of the Desert Garden Arena. Never fought in a fancy place before. Battista was in his corner, dancing around, taunting the crowd."

Donovan imagined the Kid's bloodied, beaten body bouncing on the taut canvas in the deafening arena. Battista stood over Kelly, watching the Kid's eyes dim.

"This is why you never talk about it?" asked Donovan.

"Yeah," mourned Kelly. He wet his lips and continued. "It wasn't losing, so much as it was the way I lost…nothing to be proud of."

"So why did you quit? It was only one fight, you were in your prime…"

"They'd made their money on me. I wasn't worth much to them after that. One thing you got to understand is that to people in that line of work there's nothin' like making a ton of cash on someone who's unbeaten."

"What ever happened to Battista?"

"Probably got mixed up in some mess like me. I took my share from the fight and disappeared. Spent some time around Denver, and got into trouble on my own."

"What kind of trouble?"

"I started drinking and gambling myself. Met this young prostitute. We hit it off real nice like and talked about leaving town together—maybe getting married and settling down someplace."

"But you never did?"

"No. Everything happened pretty fast when her pimp found out. I caught him in an alley, giving her the once over. All I could think of was my father. I hit him one too many times. Expected to spend the rest of my days in prison, but the cops figured I did them a favor. They told me to get out of town real fast."

"And the girl?"

Kelly didn't say anything.

"Well, then, what about boxing?"

"My life up until then had been boxing…kinda funny how it was the thing that caused the most misery in my life," explained Kelly, as he ran his broken fingers across his lips. "I finally made my

way back here. Watched the young kids at the VFW now and then—probably watched you at some time or another."

"You see any prospects?" Donovan asked.

"Some that could have been good with a little work. Most had problems with their left—probably like you, not liking to be hit. Boxing is more than putting on sixteen-ounce gloves and punching the crap out of your friends. The sport is dying. There aren't many like old Pops, who could teach a kid everything to survive in the ring."

Donovan toyed with a new napkin, scratching out his version of shorthand. "It all bothers you though, the loss of people like Pops, the sport…?"

"No. It died for me a long time ago." Kelly smiled as Donovan folded the pile of napkins and neatly tucked them into his pocket. "You're finished?"

"There's more?"

"Sure, kid. I have lots of stories," Kelly softly replied. He scowled at the blank look on Donovan's face. "So. What'll it be?"

"Maybe another story would be good," replied Donovan, with an affectionate smile. "I'll get us some more coffee and napkins."

THũnder änd LightNing

 Whenever she visited her older sister, Hattie Mae Hollis, Aunt Clare always told Donovan about how love and tragedy were inseparable. As he drove her across the old bridge, up the steep hill, past the solitary pine tree that overlooked the river and town, Aunt Clare would begin the story.

"To think what poor Hattie's been through all these years, first losing her daughter, Liane, and then her granddaughter, Tara all because of that old fool she's married to. His heart has more holes than his head."

Aunt Clare would point out the lightning-scarred tree, whose rust-colored skin was charred and split, that she called the Lovers' Tree after the young couples who found refuge beneath its draping green canopy. "I remember this place from when I was a girl. There were seven or eight trees along the cliff there, but they're all disappearing," she said, pointing at the decaying stumps. "I can't imagine Allegory Falls without lovers' trees."

"Don't worry," replied Donovan, showing Aunt Clare the seedlings in the tall grass. "New ones are emerging." She seemed momentarily pleased, but her thoughts turned back to the Hollis women. As soon as they passed the tree and rounded the hairpin curve, Aunt Clare started reminiscing.

Liane, Hattie Mae's daughter, had gotten pregnant just after she turned seventeen. Charles Hollis, Liane's father, was furious, and claimed that the Hollis family name had been tarnished forever by Liane and her boyfriend, Jeb Washburn. From then on, old man Hollis never let Liane forget her mistake, making her life miserable every chance he got. Jeb showed up before Tara was born and asked for Liane's hand. Hollis was sitting in a rocker on the porch, fixing his muskrat traps. He stared at Jeb coldly.

"I'll see you in hell first," the old man said, pulling a worn-barreled Colt automatic he got during the war from his overalls. Spitting tobacco from the side of his mouth, Charles touched off a round. He laughed as a wide-eyed, white-faced Jeb lay sprawled in the grass. "Next time, I won't aim so high," said the old man, just as Liane and Hattie burst through the front door.

Jeb was halfway to the county road when Hattie, holding her sobbing daughter, said her piece. "Charles Hollis, you're the biggest, most insensitive jackass I've ever known, and I've known a lot! If you weren't so damned worried about your good name, you'd let that nice boy marry Liane."

"That boy's no good," he sulked, turning his back on Hattie. "The girl ain't much better for that matter either, but I'll be damned if they ever marry." He bounded off the steps with his traps and disappeared into the woods.

Tara pushed open the door to her grandmother's room and raced to the end of the bed, as the rumbling and flashing of a late summer night's thunderstorm rattled the shutters. She gently tugged at the end of the bedspread so as not to startle her grandmother. A dark haired, muddy eyed girl, near seven, Tara Hollis had lived with her grandparents after Liane disappeared one night six years ago.

"What's the matter dear," asked Grandma Hattie groggily, "bad dream?"

Tara crawled under the covers at the end of the bed up to the pillow her grandma was fluffing for her. Grandma Hattie's room was separate from Grandpa's. It was small, simple and smelled like lavender. The bed was metal with brass corner posts and rose patterns on the headboard. Tara snuggled her head into her grandmother's bosom.

"Tell me, child, what's the matter?" asked Hattie, kissing Tara on the head.

"Scared," Tara replied, wrapping her arms around Grandma

Hattie's fleshy waist.

"Bad dream or just the storm?" asked Hattie.

"Both," replied Tara. Hattie held Tara and stroked her long black hair, like she had with Liane when she was little and would climb into Hattie's bed.

"I know. I miss your mama, too," said Hattie. "But someday we will see her again. She loved you very much."

"Tell me a story, Grandma," said Tara, yawning.

"Would you like to hear a story that I used to tell on nights like this when your mama was a little girl?" Tara nodded and smiled as they slid beneath the covers a little further.

"This is the story of why thunder and lightning always come together. One day a handsome young man was walking in the woods along a river. As it happened, there was a beautiful young woman walking in the forest on the other side of the river. She had long black hair and brown eyes, just like you," said Grandma Hattie.

"What happened?" asked Tara.

"They saw each other, and it was love at first sight."

"What's love at first sight?"

"Well, it's when you get to a certain age. You look at someone and you know you have to be together, forever," smiled Hattie.

"Like my mama and papa?"

"Yes, I think that happened to your mama and Jeb."

"And to you, Grandma?"

Hattie had to stop and think a moment. Why had she married Charles Hollis, the boastful, proud, arrogant old man who thought women were put on earth to do the bidding of men? He hadn't changed in the forty years they had been married and surely wasn't likely to change anytime soon.

"I suppose so, child," she said softly. "So, the two stood there looking at each other, filling their hearts until they could no longer stand being apart. The river was far too deep to wade across, and far too swift to swim across, so Lightning, the young man, told the pretty young girl he could shoot a lightning bolt

from his eyes and make the tree fall across the river so they could be together."

"Was she afraid?" asked Tara.

"No. The young girl told him that she had thunder in her

heart and when she released it, it would shake the hills and stones would roll down into the water and form a bridge." Hattie stroked Tara's hair and watched her eyes grow heavier.

"Go on, Grandma," Tara said, curling up closer to her grandmother.

"Well, Thunder opened her heart and Lightning opened his eyes wide. The mountain shook and stones began to fall into the river. Lightning hit the tree, causing it to fall, and the tree and stones came together and made a perfect bridge. The two lovers came together in the middle of the river and their two hearts joined and they never became separated again. And that is why thunder and lightning always come together." She finished as rumbling and flashes of light shook the windows of the house.

Grandma Hattie told that story to Tara many times while she was growing up. The years passed and Tara grew to be the picture of Liane, a tall, slender young woman with pendulum-like black hair and eyes like dark pools of water.

Like her mother, Tara Hollis was in love. She knew it from the first time she met Jack Hamilton crossing the narrow, single-lane bridge, the color of burnt sugar, which arched across the river. The creosote wood deck was worn and grooved, and rippled like cards being shuffled when vehicles passed over it. The mellifluous rhythm of wood against steel skimmed across the water, through the groves of cottonwood trees that lined the bank, rising over the rimrocks of a jagged bluff where a solitary pine tree stood.

Jack was a year older than Tara. A shy young man, he seemed to melt into his surroundings. But to Tara, he was never invisible. Something magical happened when their eyes first met and every time they looked at each other.

The Lovers' Tree became Jack and Tara's refuge. A waxy, red-orange tapestry of decaying pine needles cushioned them as they leaned against the tree near the edge of the river. For hours they would sit, holding hands, and tell each other stories and dream of the day they would be together forever.

Tara rushed through the back door into the kitchen where Grandma Hattie was preparing dinner.

"Where you been, Tara? If your grandfather's supper is late, there'll be hell to pay."

"There's always hell to pay, Grandma," replied Tara, grabbing the biscuit pan from the top of the cook stove and sliding it into the oven.

"Watch your tongue. If he ever heard you talk like that, he'd skin you alive," said Hattie, swatting playfully at Tara with a dish-towel.

"How come you put up with so much?" Tara stood behind her grandmother at the sink and started rubbing her shoulders and neck, as she often did when they worked together in the kitchen.

"I don't know, some men are like that. When they're courting, they tell you how they can't live without you, and afterward, they act like they don't want to live with you. One day you're a princess, and before you know it..."

Tara looked long at her grandmother. "Why didn't you leave, then?"

Hattie did not answer. "Watch the biscuits, if you burn—"

"I know, I know. There'll be hell to pay."

Charles Hollis's truck rumbled up the drive and settled into the depression worn from years of going to and from his job as a boilerman at the local mill. The rickety door slammed. He clomped up the steps and kicked off his boots without greeting Tara or Hattie.

"What's for dinner?" he demanded.

"Chicken, Pa," said Hattie, putting a bowl of peas on the table.

"Biscuits, too? Hope they ain't burnt like before," he said, washing his hands with a pumice bar at the kitchen sink.

"They're perfect," said Tara.

The old man didn't say anything as they sat down to the table and passed around the food. Then he looked at Tara.

"Talked to Joe Starks today. He said he's seen you down by the river a lot lately."

"I like to take walks, Grandfather," Tara replied nervously.

"With who?" he asked sternly.

The room was quiet except for his munching and smacking. Hattie and Tara looked at one another. Hattie tilted her head towards the old man, signaling Tara to answer him before he started fussing even more.

"Jack Hamilton."

"Bill Hamilton's boy?" asked Hattie. "Why, if he's anything like his folks, he must be—"

"Not worth a tinker's damn," snorted the old man.

"Oh, Pa," said Hattie, "they're a nice family. What's the matter with you?"

"I've told you what I think. Now, I'm going to tell you something else," he said, looking at Tara. "You stay away from him, you hear?"

Tara's face became long and dark as she stared down at her plate, drawing figure eights in her mashed potatoes.

"Charles, I don't see what harm there is in it," Hattie boldly said. "I've met the young man…he's quite pleasant. He thinks a lot of Tara. Perhaps we could have him over for dinner and you—" She was interrupted.

"I said my piece. The girl is to stay away from him," he barked.

"Besides, she has her chores to keep her plenty busy." He pushed his chair away from the table and left the kitchen. A long silence followed.

Hattie looked at Tara compassionately in the silent language they had developed when the old man was in the house. Her grandmother took her hand and kissed it. Tara hung her head, and her tears dropped onto the worn wood floor.

The weeks passed. Hollis couldn't watch Tara every minute and her grandmother made excuses for her on occasion. "She's running an errand for me, so just calm down, Pa." The charade ended one August afternoon. The trees around the Hollis place flailed in the darkening sky. "Better get the chickens in," the old man commanded Hattie, "there's a helluva storm brewin'."

That night at the dinner table, the three ate in silence. A gush of wind shot through the kitchen door, blowing the napkins off the table. When Tara bent down to pick them up, the old man noticed something in her hair.

"What's this?" he snapped, pulling pine needles from her hair. "You been up to that tree by the river again, haven't you?"

"No she hasn't, Pa," Tara's grandmother said quickly. "They probably blew off one of the trees around here when she was doing her chores."

"Sit down, girl," he growled. "You two must take me for some kind of fool. These are pine nee-dles. All we have 'round here are cottonwoods, ash and alder. They ain't nothin' alike."

"Oh, what do you know,"

said Hattie faintly.

"I sure as hell know how to put an end to this nonsense," the old man angrily said. "I'll be damned if she'll end up a slut like her mother!"

"Watch your mouth," Hattie said sharply. "I swear your tongue was made by the devil himself. You should be ashamed, Charles Hollis!"

"In the morning, have your bags packed, miss. You're going to live with your Aunt Sadie," the old man shouted as he stormed into the living room.

"You can't be serious, Charles," said Hattie. "Your sister lives in the middle of nowhere!" Aunt Sadie had a ranch in the panhandle of Texas, miles from the nearest town.

The old man just stared at Hattie with dead aim.

"You're trying to drive Tara away, the same way you did Liane," she yelled.

The rest of the evening Tara stayed in her room, looking out at the dark sky. She paced up and down, her bare feet squeaking across the freshly waxed floor. Grandma Hattie came into the room and sat on the edge of the bed. Tara laid her head in her grandmother's lap.

"If I thought I could change your stubborn grandfather's mind, I would," Hattie pined, stroking Tara's brow.

"I don't want to go to Aunt Sadie's," moaned Tara.

Hattie's face drooped. She bent and kissed Tara. "This one is for me, this one is for your mother, and this one is for Jack," she said, giving her three warm kisses. Hattie reached into her apron. "Here, take this. I've been saving this pin money for a rainy day. Looks like my timing is right," she added, as the heavy drops began to pelt the window.

Tara looked at her grandmother and smiled as the tears rolled off her nose. "But Grandma—"

"You're wasting time, child," said Hattie. "Go on."

Hattie helped Tara pack her bag. They waited until the old man was sound asleep in his chair. Tara quietly called Jack and arranged to meet him at the bridge. "Now go, before your grandfather wakes up and gets some crazy notion," Hattie said.

Tara hugged her grandmother a final time, tiptoed past her grandfather, and carefully eased off the porch so the steps wouldn't squeak. She turned to wave to Hattie and then ran down the red clay road to meet Jack.

"One last time before we go," Tara whispered to Jack as they walked hand in hand along the oiled deck of the bridge, listening to the rippling waters beneath their feet. The boiling, leaden skies of August were kissing the rims of the mountains when they reached the old pine. Their clothes dropped beneath the tree in a shallow where the knotted roots pushed beyond the edge of the cliff and lay exposed. The wind covered them with a layer of needles.

With her hand on Jack's heart, Tara told him her grandmother's story of Thunder and Lightning. Jack gazed deeply into her eyes as the words danced from her heart. They leaned against one another as the warm scent of pine filled the air. The heavens rumbled and a single brilliant, fiery bolt flashed at the solitary tree.

"That was the last anyone ever heard of Tara and Jack," said Aunt Clare as she and Donovan pulled up Hattie Mae's driveway. She glanced up at the sky. "Looks like a storm's brewing," she said, walking up the steps of the old porch.

The
Color Orange

 "What are you laughing about?" asked Donovan, suddenly swerving over the center line on the old highway. The back of his old Chevy overflowed with rickety pieces of furniture.

"I don't know how anyone could possibly miss seeing *that* sign," chuckled Aunt Clare, as she and Donovan hurtled past Art and Gabriella.

"Since when has anyone paid attention to those signs?" replied Donovan. "You know the color orange is only a suggestion. And speed is nine-tenths of defensive driving in Allegory Falls anyway."

"What's the other part?"

"Good brakes."

Aunt Clare sighed. "I worry about those two—the way they seem to appear from nowhere. Don't you find them a little funny? You know, kind of quirky?"

"Odd, perhaps," replied Donovan as he craned his neck over the seat and backed the truck to the door of the long, rectangular shack. "But not funny."

The shack stood in the far corner of the field behind the boarding house and was once used to store apple crates when the orchard was productive. It had looked like a child's house of cards before Aunt Clare had Donovan start repairs so Art Steen could live there. Now it was covered from top to bottom with rolled roofing, a desert tan color, and studded with large-headed galvanized nails that glimmered like sequins in the sun.

Art Steen was Allegory Falls's undisputed king of trash. His fortune was as lamentable as what he collected, but for the brief time he lived in Magruder's shack, he never appeared more content.

Aunt Clare stood with her hands on her hips, giving orders to

Donovan as to what she wanted done with the old shed. "Someone has to look out for the less fortunate in life. Never forget that."

Donovan shook his head. "We have an artist and his dog, some distant cousin neither of us remembers who, by the way, scares the hell out of everyone the way he peers out his window, and a few that can't pay their rent on time. The boarding house is looking more like a halfway house every day. And now Art and Gabriella. Who next?"

"You needn't worry about that," answered Aunt Clare. "And just remember, it wasn't my idea to bring that dog and his artist into the house. You know the cat hasn't been the same since." Aunt Clare turned and sat in the antique rocker. "Now hurry and finish with the work. Art will be here soon."

———

Art Steen smiled at Gabriella and bent down to pick up a discarded shard from the twisted stalks of weeds and grasses that grew along the highway.

"This will do just fine," he said to Gabriella. "This will do just fine." With Gabriella by his side, and never more than a half-day's journey from the shed Donovan had renovated for them, the two spent their days looking for what would "do just fine."

Near sunset Art and Gabriella walked to their new home. Clumps of fescue grass below the stoop served as their welcome mat. Donovan and Aunt Clare approached.

"It's not much, but it's liveable," Donovan said apologetically.

"This'll do," replied Art. He drew his arm around Gabriella's neck and gave her a big squeeze. "Just fine."

Gabriella was an aging, mangy burro. Her once luxurious hide was covered with a puzzle of callouses from the straps that pulled the two-wheeled cart Art built. Since he hadn't used wheels of the same size, the cart listed

about two inches to one side. Donovan offered to amend the oversight, but Art just shook his head and said, "It's fine. Gabriella don't know tire size, anyway."

"You need help with any-thing," began Aunt Clare, "Donovan would be more than—"

"Nope," Art said, "we can manage real fine, Ms. Magruder."

"There are still some things Donovan needs to finish," added Aunt Clare, handing Art a basket of food.

"That'll be fine." Art set the basket on the porch and reached down to retrieve a rusty nail. He wore gloves that had holes in the thumb, index and middle fingers, and his fingers looked like little pink tongues as they probed through the grass.

"If Joseph had a cart instead of a coat," Aunt Clare said, "he'd have had yours. By the way, I have a little quilt for your burro's back, if you'd like."

Art just grinned. "Yes, I imagine he would have, at that." He blushed and turned slightly away.

"And the quilt for Gabriella, Art?" Aunt Clare insisted. "Her poor back—and it's getting much colder at night now."

"No ma'am, no quilt," droned Art. "Gabby's just fine, thanks." He slapped her smartly on the flanks.

Art had nailed, taped and wired a large Slow Moving Vehicle sign to the back of the cart at the insistence of the county sher-iff after one too many complaints by unsuspecting motorists. Art had become so safety conscious that he asked Aunt Clare to sew a miniature version of the sign on the back of his frayed denim ranch coat. But it did not deter Gabriella from running up the back of Art's heels with her sharp, asphalt-worn hooves.

Donovan helped Aunt Clare into the truck and glanced back at Art, still probing the grass.

"Why would anyone want to collect junk?" he wondered aloud.

"Someone's got to do it," replied Aunt Clare, as they pulled into the driveway of the boarding house.

"Maybe the possessed should be left alone." Donovan opened the door for Aunt Clare, as her cat streaked between her legs.

"Art is," scowled Aunt Clare. "See, I told you the cat hasn't been the same."

———

Art was a droopy man. His glowing optic orange cap had imitation wool ear flaps that fastened with velcro at the top, the kind Craving's Sporting Goods sold to hunters. Small tufts of yellowed white hair sprigged out in odd angles beneath his cap. He was always hunched over, the result of too many decades of looking at the ground.

"Sure can't miss seeing him," said Aunt Clare, looking out the kitchen window across the field to the shed, where Art was hitching Gabriella to the cart.

"Nor the accumulating mounds of trash," replied Donovan.

"They're not mounds," snapped Aunt Clare. "Why, you can hardly see them from here."

"What do you think he does with it all?" asked Donovan.

Aunt Clare grabbed a dishtowel, wiped her hands, and opened the round lid on the wood stove. She lit a match and ignited the newspaper and kindling, filling the kitchen with a whooshing sound. She slid the iron handle into the lid and pushed it over the crackling fire, and stood a moment watching the orange flames swirl over the lid.

"You're always the one who has an answer for everything," she said. "Why don't you just ask him?" Aunt Clare turned slowly and walked back to the window.

"Maybe I will," replied Donovan.

The next day, Donovan's truck bounced over the uneven ground and slowed to a stop at the shed.

"Back to finish up," he said, grabbing his tool bag from the bed of the truck.

Art adjusted his gloves, pushing his fingers together like kids do when they pray. "We're just leaving."

"Can I ask you something?" Donovan's voice crackled.

"If you have to, I reckon."

"What do you do with this stuff?" Donovan motioned to Art's piles.

"Make things and sell them," he said.

"What do you make, exactly?"

"Don't know…just things." Art moved toward the door, fidgeting with the orange cap on his head.

"Could I see them?" asked Donovan tentatively, peering through the blackened screen.

"I reckon," Art said with a mulching voice. "Come on in." He pushed the door open with his foot and pointed to the dimly lit room. "There."

Donovan stood, speechless, staring at the things Art had made. "How long have you been doing this?"

"Most of my life," mumbled Art, as he wiped his shirt sleeve across his mouth. "I guess."

"Does anyone know?"

"Sure. Plenty of folks. I sell the stuff in the next county." Art rummaged through his cupboard and found jam and butter to spread on a roll with his fingers. "Big-city people like them."

Donovan laughed. "Selling things people have already bought and trashed. It's funny." He watched Art's blank stare turn to confusion. "You know—people buying their own trash back."

"If you say so." Art sat at his makeshift table, a large spool that he had scavenged from the Rural Electric Co-op.

"These are wonderful. I've never seen anything like them."

Donovan moved around Art's creations, noticing the care he gave to each one.

"Reckon not," Art said. "That one there is Gabby."

Donovan smiled. "Looks just like her, too." Art had formed the image with wood, wire and nails. He painted it with dots and slashes and lots of vivid colors.

"Better, I think," said Art, looking at Gabby, who had stuck her head in the door.

"This you?" Donovan pointed to a bending figure with a small

tire rim for one foot and a radiator and hoses for the torso.

"I guess."

Donovan turned to him. "I like how you used a saucepan for the hat."

"Needs paint," Art answered, wiping his mouth where bits of food had lodged in his beard. "Orange."

"I can get you some," Donovan said eagerly.

"Nope. Wouldn't be the same." He paused and looked up at Donovan. "You know something? It's not how you look at things, it's how they look at you."

Donovan thought about that while Art continued to eat.

"You could sell these here."

"Already have a place to sell them." Art moved to the door and stood at the threshold.

Donovan sensed Art's anxiety and stepped outside. "Can I get you anything?"

Art just shook his head.

"Is there anything I can get Gabriella, then?"

"Don't reckon," said Art. "She ate windfalls along the road and broke wind the whole day. That's why she's outside. Doesn't need anything more."

"See you later then," said Donovan. Art stood behind the screen, looking like one of his creations.

Fall arrived, and Art disappeared in the landscape, which was carpeted in the deluge of molting aspens, cottonwoods, poplars and maples. Hunting season made Art so paranoid that he spray-painted in orange B-U-R-O down Gabriella's flanks to warn overzealous hunters. Gabriella looked like a graffiti wall where Art struggled to correctly spell the word. Afraid that wasn't enough, he also tied strips of orange flagging to Gabby's short mane and tail.

Aunt Clare stood at the kitchen window, watching Art cross the field. "Did you see what Art has done to that poor burro?"

"I offered to help," said Donovan, shifting in his chair by the wood stove. "At least I would have spelled it right."

"I think it's nonsense," said Aunt Clare. She put her glasses on and leaned over the sink closer to the window. "No hunter in his right mind would shoot at an ass—they look nothing like deer."

"You'd be surprised," replied Donovan. "That guy from St. Louis shot Tom Breechman's mule and tried to convince the game warden it was a cow moose."

"I still think it's nonsense," sighed Aunt Clare.

"Art seems to be satisfied," said Donovan. "He said this was the first year Gabriella had not been shot at, so it must work."

―――

"I don't understand how they could not see him," said Aunt Clare, with a tear in her eye. She, Donovan and three of her friends stood graveside as Father Byrnes finished reading a psalm.

"I never expected this would happen either," said Donovan as he consoled Aunt Clare. "But I always said no one pays much attention to the color orange.

Donovan stared at the headstone he and Aunt Clare had chosen. It had shoots of native grasses and wildflowers chiseled on the front, and simply read "Art Steen," since no one knew anything else about the man.

"Art would have liked it," Aunt Clare said in a broken voice.

"Yeah," replied Donovan. "You can almost see his fingers probing through those shoots of grass."

"I wish I had known more about him," sobbed Aunt Clare.

"I think we knew enough," replied Donovan.

Gabriella, who had bolted when the rifle shot reverberated through a thicket near the river, looking like a donkey on fire as the strands of orange tape billowed in the breeze, now stood in the field behind the boarding house, mangy, calloused and still listing to one side, with orange stains down her backside. Art's backside was a different story.

"I wish Art had been more cautious," Aunt Clare said, leaning on Donovan's arm.

"It wouldn't have mattered. Art had bent over one too many times. It was inevitable that the seat of his pants would give out." Donovan imagined Art's fleshy, white backside bursting out of his pants in that dark thicket. For an instant, it must have looked like the flank of a whitetail deer.

Donovan walked to the open grave and tossed Art's orange cap on the pine casket. He knew Art was somewhere still looking for that which would do him just fine.

bēatlë Boots

Itty McNeal and Cole Parish were sitting in Haig's Bar at a green felt card table when Jim 'the Knife' Smitz strutted through the door with his latest girlfriend, Rennie Nunn. Her cheap jewelry clinked like the brass bell that hung from the heavy glass door as they glided across the room, homing in on the pool table in the far corner of the bar.

Smitz had the looks—dark eyes, straight nose, full pouty mouth, and swarthy complexion—that ensorcelled the girls in Allegory Falls. His hair was dark and wet, and smelled of Vitalis; his wiry body was vacuum-packed into black jeans, and from his cuffs extended the pointed toes of black high-heeled boots made popular by the Beatles. Smitz had Evan's Boot and Saddle Shop put taps on the heels, which not only kept him from wearing down the outside of his heels but also served as his personal calling card.

"How many pairs of those boots do you think he has?" pondered Itty. Parish hung his head, watching each step Smitz took. "I bet he has enough in his closet to last him a lifetime. He'll go to his grave wearing those things. Even ol' man Nussbaum at the funeral parlor wouldn't have the nerve to pull them off his dead corpse for fear of running into him in the hereafter."

The Knife enjoyed his role as crown prince of Allegory Falls's taverns, card parlors, pool halls and gaunt women who clung to him. He acquired his nickname when he was a kid. After putting on his first pair of Beatle Boots, he had tucked a knife inside his right boot, but it didn't remain out of sight for long. After slicing up one of his classmates in study hall, Smitz was sent to reform school for three years. He perfected his trade there, at an old billiard table in the day room.

Smitz walked past McNeal and Parish, giving them a quick, sneering glance. A group of high school kids were playing a game of cowboy pool when Smitz swaggered to the table and slapped a quarter down. The sound barely dissipated when the wide-eyed teens leaned their cues against the back wall and exited like a bevy of flushed pheasants.

"Hey, the missing Beatle has arrived," McNeal said loudly, elbowing Parish. "You want his autograph?"

Parish nudged McNeal with his foot and whispered, "Keep it down. He'll hear you."

"So what? What's he gonna do?"

"For starters, he carries a knife, and secondly, he's a lot bigger than you. He scares me," Parish mumbled.

"Your grandmother scares you," retorted McNeal in disgust.

"Hey," barked Smitz. McNeal turned and glared at him. "Yeah, you two worms. Get over here and give me a game. It seems the boys were late for their milk and cookies."

Parish looked like a cur dog about to be flogged. He pulled on McNeal's sleeve in a pathetic attempt to deter him.

"C'mon," said McNeal, knocking Parish's sweaty hand away. "We'll play a rack and then leave."

"I can't play pool," whimpered Parish.

"You're pathetic," snapped McNeal. "You can watch–maybe you'll learn something." He set his empty glass on the bar and walked to the cue holder, taking his jacket off as he went.

Smitz stood with one foot against the wall, one arm slung over Rennie's shoulder. A cigarette dangled from his lower lip as he grinned at Itty, exhaled and drew the smoke back through his nostrils. "You rack, little man."

McNeal's muscles constricted. "8-ball?" he growled. At five feet two inches in work boots, McNeal was an easy target for such derision.

Smitz writhed his snaky frame in some pre-game ritual. "Yeah, and make it tight. I hate squirrels who can't rack 'em right." He twisted his neck until it rippled like the sounds of balls landing in the table's pockets.

Parish skirted the far wall and parked himself next to Rennie on the curved wooden bench below the large rear window.

"What are you staring at?" scowled Rennie. McNeal could almost hear Parish's bones pop from the tension as he quickly left the bench.

"I'll play the both of you," said Smitz. "Hell, I'll even let you break first." He lit another cigarette with a flick of his Zippo.

"You break," said Itty, handing the cue to Parish.

Smitz exhaled another cloud of smoke. "Let's make it a fiver to start with."

"We're playing for money?"

"It's okay," Itty said to Parish. "I'll cover your end."

Parish placed the cue ball on the table and shuddered, remembering that Sam Hotchkins once refused to play the Knife for money. Two days later it took sixty-three stitches to close the dollar sign Smitz had carved into his chest.

A faint "chink" broke the silence as the tip of Parish's cue slipped off center, sending the ball caroming off the right-hand cushion.

"Nice break." Smitz gulped his beer and waved the empty glass at Donovan. "Now pull up your panties and this time, get it right."

Parish stood behind the cue ball, poised to redeem himself. McNeal sat on the bench eyeing Rennie, who busied herself filing her long nails.

Smitz laughed at Parish's feeble break and proceeded to run

twelve straight. He cocked his head, strutted around the table, and looked at Itty slumped on the bench. "Another fiver you losers don't sink a ball!"

"Don't have another five," blurted Parish, collapsing on the bench between McNeal and Rennie.

"What the hell, you can owe me."

Parish kicked nervously at McNeal's feet. Being in debt to Smitz was more costly than losing straight up. Everyone in Allegory Falls knew how Mick Gilbert ended up owing money to Smitz after a high-stakes match. For the next four months, Gilbert became Smitz's personal auto-teller. All Smitz had to do was to stick out his hand and snap his fingers and fresh bills would appear. When Gilbert ran out of money, his wife Lisa went begging to Smitz. "You deserve that deadbeat." Smitz slapped her across the face with the back of his hand. "Tell him he still owes me and I'll be looking for him." The Gilberts slipped quietly out of town that night with what possessions they could pile into their AMC Pacer. No one had heard from them since.

The blue chalk on the leather tip kissed the cue ball, spattering a tiny dust cloud that quickly settled on the table. Parish followed every rotation until it collided with the 5-ball. The 13-ball wobbled gently and settled precariously on the edge of the left side pocket.

"Damn!" bellowed Smitz, slamming the blunt end of the stick against the floor. The sound reverberated off the walls and high ceiling of the bar like a tympani drum. "Your turn, runt," he snarled at Itty. He turned angrily and walked to the bench, where Rennie consoled him.

McNeal took the stick from Parish and approached the table. He knew he could hold his own with Smitz—he could read Haig's high-legged table like a book when he bent over to aim his cue. He strode around the table as he sized up his plan of attack. Parish breathed a deep sigh of relief that he and Itty were not yet indebted to Smitz.

"Five ball, side pocket," Itty calmly said, gliding the cue

through his fingers.

"Then what?" goaded Smitz, running his hand along Rennie's thigh.

"The 13-ball you missed," McNeal needled.

Facing the prospect of having to part with money, Smitz shouted, "Double or nothing," in the middle of McNeal's backstroke.

"You're on!" said Itty instantly.

Parish's mouth dropped, and he melted into the wooden bench. McNeal flashed him a reassuring glance, knowing he had Smitz where he wanted him, but Parish's eyes were closed.

"Well, that's ten you owe us," said McNeal quietly, as the cue ball slowly came to rest against the back cushion. Parish, an ashen lump on the bench, stared in disbelief.

Smitz wore his patented smirk. "Nice game. Let's play another, for a ten spot. You seem to be lucky today."

"We have to go," blurted Parish, getting up from the bench.

"I wasn't talking to you," lashed Smitz, not taking his eyes off McNeal.

Knowing how devious Smitz could be, McNeal carefully watched him rack the balls. "It's too loose," McNeal said, staring down at the turn-of-the-century slate table whose lush felt was perfectly brushed.

"So it is," Smitz grumbled, re-racking the balls.

"Can't believe my luck," muttered Itty, chalking his stick and moving around the table after draining eleven straight.

"Tell you what," Smitz said, crushing his cigarette out on the oiled wood floor. "Double or nothing again—I'm feeling generous today."

McNeal stretched his body across the green felt to bank the eight-ball. He didn't answer Smitz.

"What's the matter, no guts?"

"Your money." Itty nailed the cue ball with one last forceful stroke. He walked to the cue holder, pressed his stick into the brass catches and dusted his hands on his jeans.

Smitz rifled his pockets with difficulty. "Here," he snarled. "Buy yourself some high heels." He slapped a twenty on the table.

"That was thirty," said McNeal.

Smitz tossed another ten on the table. "We'll meet again." He curled up on the bench with Rennie, waiting for some other mark to arrive at the table. "We'll definitely meet again." Those words resounded with each step as McNeal and Parish exited Haig's.

It was weeks before Smitz's words came true. McNeal and Parish entered Haig's after slushing along the wet, puddled gravel of the alley. The tables were full of old men with ravaged faces and white hair, some smoking, some drinking, some quarreling. The area near the pool table was teeming with young kids, languid from Haig's atmosphere, sipping Coke and Orange Crush. It was all part of the Friday night ritual, acted out of small-town boredom.

Itty and Cole sat at the bar, ordered a pint each, and resumed their debate about the rumors that International Sawmill was on the verge of closure. Near the end of their first beer, Parish felt an involuntary quiver crawl up his pant leg and quickly un-zip his spine.

"Smitz is here," he whispered to Itty.

"So what?"

"Remember, he said he'd meet up with you again, and I don't think he was talking about a rematch."

"Relax," said McNeal, arching his tired back and shoulders. He turned his head toward the pool table. It was difficult to see through the throng of onlookers, but spotting Smitz's boots in a sea of tennis shoes and cowboy boots was as easy as spotting an elephant in a cow pasture. "Yep. Smitz is here, alright."

"Can we just go to the Workman?" Parish pleaded.

"And what," replied Itty, "watch the wallpaper peel or listen to another of Kelly's boxing stories? No thanks."

"Eagles has a live band. There'll be plenty of girls."

"None my height, but if it makes you feel better, we'll leave," McNeal said, licking beer foam from his upper lip. "Just stop sniveling."

"Thanks," Parish replied. "And I'm not sniveling. I'm just being cautious, that's all."

"Cautious?" mocked McNeal. "Smitz is perfectly content where he's at. Just look—some unsuspecting kid doesn't know he's about to play the monkey."

Parish and McNeal hopped off their stools and made their way out the door, down the chiseled stoop of the old brick building

and around the corner to the narrow canyon of the alley, lit only by the lights from Haig's rear window.

"Well, well," rang a familiar voice from the shadows. "What do we have here?" Smitz staggered from too many beers, Rennie doing her best to keep him upright. They emerged from the dark recesses of the alley and slowly made their way toward McNeal and Parish. Rennie's frangible peroxide hair glistened in the light as she clung to Smitz. "Jimmy has something to say," she told them.

"We don't want any trouble," blurted Parish, practically standing on top of McNeal.

"Shut up," Smitz slurred. He

grabbed Parish by the throat and forced him to the ground. Parish made hissing sounds like air escaping from steam pipes as Smitz tightened his grip.

"What do you want, Smitz?" growled McNeal.

"I want my money back, that's what."

Rennie stood over Parish, gloating. "Yeah, Jimmy wants his money back—the money you stole from him."

"C'mon," said McNeal, "I won fair and square, but if you want the money that bad, I'll give it to you. Just lay off him!" He reached into his pocket and tossed it at Smitz. "Here, take it."

Rennie fluttered like a chicken picking up the bills scattered across the alley.

"You know, little man," began Smitz in a cold voice, "you should have learned to lose."

Not thinking, McNeal turned his back on Smitz to help Parish, who was still gasping. The temptation for Smitz was too great to resist. He reached down quickly for his knife, staggered sideways, and drew the blade from his boot. The sound of the blade locking into position shivered through Parish as he clung to McNeal, inadvertently pulling him to the ground. The blade glimmered hypnotically as Smitz whirled his knife in the darkness of the alley.

———

"Now you've done it!" squealed Parish.

"Shut up!" yelled McNeal. He knelt beside Smitz's unconscious body, trying to dodge Rennie's flailing arms.

"You bastards'll pay for this," she screamed.

Smitz had thrashed about wildly, losing his footing and falling against the brick building. The knife disappeared under him.

"Geez," whimpered Parish, "there's a lot of blood." He quickly backed away, out of the light.

"Relax!" McNeal shouted as Rennie began sobbing hysterically. "He'll live—it's only a flesh wound."

Rennie saw the knife under Smitz's side and reached for it. McNeal quickly knocked her hand away and tossed the knife into the darkness.

"Let's go." Parish pulled at McNeal.

"I want my money back." McNeal reached toward Rennie.

"What are you doing, you little shit?" she squealed when Itty grabbed the tiny purse suspended from her shoulder by a gold-plated chain. "Leave me alone! Here, here's your damn money," she said, throwing it at Itty.

"Just wait, Jimmy will get you for this! You hear me? Jimmy will get you!" Rennie yelled as Itty and Parish made their way down the alley.

"He will find you," said Parish. "Then what will you do?"

McNeal worked the night shift at the sawmill, operating the chipper, which ground tailing butts and trim slabs from logs that were used for fuel for boilers and kilns, pressboard sheathing and cardboard boxes. The waste material traveled on a chain-driven conveyor before it dropped into the bowels of the chipper. The noise from the machinery was deafening as it pulverized the waste material into thin-wafered chips.

A butt had lodged sideways in the chute, and McNeal struggled to free it with his pry bar when a hand seized his shoulder. His heart jumped as he spun around. Dropping his pry bar, he stared, white-eyed, into Smitz's smirking face.

"You knew I'd come for you," bellowed Smitz at the top of his lungs, the saliva stretched like rubber bands in the corners of his bloodless lips. He shoved McNeal against the side of the chute, while tailings rushed by his head, cascading off the end of the conveyor. The vitreous light above the catwalk danced over the edge of Smitz's knife.

"Wait," yelled Itty as Smitz whipped his blade through Itty's safety rope. "This isn't…"

"Wait, nothing," screamed Smitz, crouching over McNeal. He pushed Itty further over the chute. "The time for waiting is over," added Smitz as he lunged toward McNeal.

"Hey, McNeal," said Floyd Carlsen, the millwright, as the two punched the time clock, ending another graveyard shift. "Some guy was looking for you earlier…he find you?"

McNeal spun around, standing cheek to cheek with Floyd.

"Boy, you're jumpy tonight." Floyd backed away from him. "What's the matter?"

"Nothing…unfinished business…it's taken care of now."

"Hey, did you get a look at those boots the guy had on? The funniest things I ever saw," laughed Carlsen.

"You get a good look at him?" McNeal asked.

"No, I was working on an undercarriage. All I saw was those boots. I just pointed him in your direction with my leg," Floyd said, slapping Itty on the back as he made his way to his truck. "Funniest things, those boots," chuckled Floyd as he opened the door. "See you, McNeal."

"Sure, see you, Floyd." McNeal climbed into his Bonneville, his heart sputtering like the stuck valve in the car's engine. He wound his way through the empty mill yard, past a semi backing up to the hopper for another load of chips. A chill blanketed Itty as he paused before turning onto the highway.

"You gonna drink it or spill it?" Donovan asked, noticing that McNeal was caught in some daydream.

"Huh? Oh, sorry, Donovan." McNeal shook his head.

Donovan leaned over the bar. "Anything the matter?"

"No, everything's just fine." He grinned at Donovan. "Just fine."

It had been seven months since Smitz lurched over McNeal with his knife, and no one except Rennie seemed to miss him. But Itty would never forget Smitz. He toyed with his beer glass, and wondered what fate Smitz met that night. Did he end up as a sheet of particle board? Or a cardboard box that would one day store, in the dark recesses of a closet, the odds and ends of life, like Beatle Boots?

Riding High

 Ilyeana Mantolova walked the final way up the road, a long, steady grade, to Magruder's Boarding House, with Aunt Clare's cat following her closely. Ilyeana stood briefly at the iron gate, catching her breath, as Abdullah rubbed his dusty head on her blue spider-veined ankles. Ilyeana looked up at the rusty spires on the cupolas of the three-storied house and exhaled.

"Hope they don't get me room on top floor," she said, closing the gate behind her. Abdullah danced up the walkway and onto the porch. Ilyeana was a behemothian, red-haired Russian with a pretty complexion, naturally rosy cheeks and eyes as dark blue as the sky before sunset. She arrived in Allegory Falls with the distinction of being its first mail-order bride.

She walked slowly up the steps of the house. Aunt Clare, wearing her finest blue dress, with a freshly perfumed handkerchief tucked into her sleeve, met her at the door and smiled brightly. Ilyeana smiled back. She was wearing a plain black dress and a wide-brimmed, pale pink hat.

"Welcome," said Aunt Clare, as Ilyeana passed through the threshold and set down her big suitcase, the kind that folds in half and has wide leather straps with big brass buckles. "We've been expecting you." Donovan smiled his greeting and eyed the monstrous case.

"Thank you," Ilyeana carefully replied with a heavy, audible sigh. "This place is hard to find. No one knows your Allegory Falls." Except for difficulty pronouncing w's and th's, her English was good. Aunt Clare introduced her nephew and instructed him to take Ilyeana's bag to her room.

"Thank you, no," she said, pulling the bag sharply from him. "I carry. Where is my room, please?"

Aunt Clare and Donovan noticed that her warm expression suddenly changed when she was told that her room was on the top floor.

Aunt Clare smiled. "Donovan will help you."

"Thank you, no," she said, looking up the steep, wallpapered canyon of the house. "When I meet my Ben?" She moved toward the stairs.

"Mr. Cutter will be here for dinner at seven," answered Aunt Clare. Abdullah shot out of her arms and up the stairs, nearly tripping Ilyeana.

"Good. I rest then," said Ilyeana, trudging up the stairs, panting the entire way.

"Seems pleasant enough," Aunt Clare said to Donovan. "Looks tired though. I wonder why she didn't call from the bus station."

Donovan shrugged. "Maybe I should bring the big chair up from the cellar for the dining table."

"Good idea." Aunt Clare brushed Abdullah's hair from her dress.

At 6:45, Aunt Clare, Donovan and Ben Cutter were seated around the cherry dining table. Aunt Clare had set out her finest china and silver, two cloisonné candle holders and an arrangement of roses with balsam sprigs. Ben was seated so he would be directly across from Ilyeana.

Ilyeana's door slammed. Slow, steady steps gathered momentum and echoed down the narrow stairway. Ilyeana shot past the dining room, stopping just short of the front door. Donovan rose, led her into the dining room and formally introduced her to Ben.

They smiled at each other, Ilyeana looking down, Ben stretching his neck to look up at his bride-to-be.

Ben Cutter was in his early fifties, a small, almost anorexic man of average looks. No one would guess from his appearance that he was an accomplished stone mason. He bowed and took Ilyeana's hand to kiss it. She blushed daintily and looked at the spot he kissed.

The big chair creaked when Ilyeana sat down across from Ben. Aunt Clare had helped so many love-struck couples in the past that she recognized love at first sight when she saw it. Ben and Ilyeana stared at one another the entire meal without saying much, but Aunt Clare knew plenty of words were spoken silently between their hearts.

After dinner, the four retired into the big vaulted living room, filled with Aunt Clare's antique furniture. Ilyeana and Ben sat next to each other on the sofa, across from Aunt Clare and Donovan. Ilyeana's robust figure sank into the rose-colored floral uphol-stery, causing Ben to look equally tall. Aunt Clare broke the silence.

"Tell us how your romance began."

The pleasure showed plainly on their faces.

"I tell," said Ilyeana, excitedly. "When the old Soviet Union break up, many girls in Moscow hear about a business that can find men from all over the world who are looking for good wives. I make good wife."

Ben nodded enthusiastically.

"I see Ben's picture on the wall. I like his face, so I take his picture and we begin to write."

Donovan remembered when Ben first received Ilyeana's pic-ture. He raced all over town that morning, showing it to everyone.

"Sounds lovely," said Aunt Clare. "But are there no men to marry in Russia?"

"Plenty of men, once. Many went to Siberia and never come back. My grandfather and father. Ones there now have no work and drink too much," said Ilyeana soberly.

Aunt Clare's face saddened. She asked Ilyeana to tell them more about herself and her family.

"I worked carrying coal on my back from railroad cars to city and sell. I make living because I carry lots," she said. "No future in Russia. When Ben asked me to marry, I come. We have been writing for two years now. Much paperwork is required."

"What about your family?" asked Aunt Clare. "It must be hard to leave them."

"When my mother die, I had no more family except for cousin." Donovan and Ben sat listening to the two women talk. "My cousin, Natasha, marry rich American man like I do," Ilyeana said proudly.

Ben's face turned as gray as the cold ashes in the fireplace. Aunt Clare and Donovan stared at him. He may have been rich by Russian standards, but he was living paycheck to paycheck, like everyone else. He had saved for over a year to get Ilyeana to Allegory Falls.

"A lot of rich Americans, yes?" Ilyeana asked, eagerly.

Donovan stared at Ben. "There are some, yes." That seemed to please Ilyeana, who patted Ben on the leg.

"Where did you learn English?" asked Aunt Clare, hoping to change the subject.

"My mother teach me to read and write when I was young," replied Ilyeana. "I learn good, yes?"

Aunt Clare nodded her head and grinned. "Yes, very good."

"I cannot marry rich man, prince, without good English."

At the word prince, everyone sat up a little straighter.

"Allow me to clear this misunderstanding up. It's rather easy to explain," said Ben, surprised at the conclusions Ilyeana drew from his letters.

"What?" Ilyeana said, frowning. "My Ben explained all this in the letters. I saved all of them." Ilyeana took a small bundle of letters from the pocket of her dress. "You explain to Ilyeana now, this…misunderstanding."

Donovan and Aunt Clare glanced at one another and frowned.

"I think Ilyeana is referring to the time I worked at Graceland for the King—you know, Presley," Ben said. He was proud that he had done stone work for Elvis's estate, and had pictures of Graceland and the King all over his office. "I sent her one of the pictures of me with Elvis." A fat Elvis in sequins, Donovan thought, might have looked like royalty to Ilyeana. And working for the King must, quite logically, make one a rich prince.

"Yes, the King," said Ilyeana proudly. "In Russia, we had no king. Only tsars." Ilyeana handed a letter and picture to Aunt Clare. It read:

> Dear Ilyeana,
> I hope this letter finds you well. I must tell you of the time I worked for "The King" at Graceland. It's a palatial house in Memphis. I'm enclosing a picture of the King. I was a lot younger then. I hope you have considered my proposal. I anxiously await your answer.
> Love,
> Ben

Donovan grinned as he read the letter. Ben was in over his head. He could explain how he had worked for Elvis, but how, he asked, did Ilyeana think he was a prince?

Ben reluctantly told them how he never had much luck making friends or meeting women. Before learning about mail order brides, he had joined A.S.S., the Anachronistic Shield Society, a group committed to resurrecting the Middle Ages. Its members assumed an identity, dressed in authentic attire, and acted out their fantasies. Before Ben began writing to Ilyeana, he drove to remote locations in the highlands of New Mexico, where groups from all over the region reenacted battles and acts of chivalry.

Donovan knew of the group, and had a hard time imagining Ben, dressed in a costume of metal and leather that probably weighed more than he, acting the part of some prince. But, Ben explained that A.S.S. had become an inextricable part of his life.

"I told Ilyeana about my costume and the weekend retreats," declared Ben.

Donovan leaned over and whispered to Aunt Clare what he was talking about. She looked confused.

"I've never heard of such a thing," she said. "Acting out fantasies in costumes…sounds like…"

"It's very popular," Donovan quickly interjected.

"You're not part of this, are you?" Aunt Clare asked.

"No! I was just pointing out that a lot of people belong to these groups. It's all innocent enough," he said.

"Costume?" bellowed Ilyeana.

"You know. The group I belong to. I explained all that in my letters," said Ben, trying to remember what he'd written.

Ilyeana passed around another letter.

> Dear Ilyeana,
> I went to another Anachronistic Society gathering. As Prince Bayreuth, I made an immediate impression on the other nobles and servants. I mentioned to them how you had brightened these past months of my life. Many said they could hardly wait to meet you and initiate you into our court. Until then…
> Love,
> Ben

"You say you are prince in the letter!" exclaimed Ilyeana, grabbing Ben's thigh. The pain drained the color from his face, and he bit his lower lip.

"I enjoy A.S.S., and the more I participate, the more I want to share that experience with Ilyeana. I guess I embellished too much," he said, looking first at Donovan and then Aunt Clare, who smiled politely.

For a moment, Ben Cutter sensed everyone understood. He nervously smiled at Ilyeana, but his smile quickly flattened. She had become quiet and her breathing seemed to stop.

"I think you need to explain it better, so Ilyeana will understand. She seems to be under some misconception with this prince-king business," said Aunt Clare innocently. "I'm not sure I understand it, myself."

"You not a prince? Not work for King?" asked Ilyeana.

"Yes…no…sort of," blurted Ben. "I can explain."

Ilyeana broke into a tirade of Russian and rose from the couch.

"Wedding is off!" She stormed from the living room, past Aunt Clare and Donovan. "No marry Ben. Lie like communist."

Ben shrank into the sofa, limp as a dishtowel. Aunt Clare followed Ilyeana upstairs, and Donovan moved next to Ben.

"I really messed this up," said Ben, "but I really do want to marry her."

"Yeah, you did," replied Donovan. "Ilyeana will forgive you once you explain this prince business so she can understand."

For three days, all was not forgiven. Ilyeana locked herself in her room, refusing to see anyone. Her sobbing echoed down the cavernous stairwell and throughout the house.

"Now what am I supposed to do?" asked Ben, as he stood on the steps of the boarding house one afternoon.

Donovan didn't give it much thought before he blurted out, "What would your alter ego, prince whatever, do?"

Ben's eyes sparkled. The answer to his problem was so simple. He turned and rushed off the porch, down the lane.

"Prince Bayreuth!" he shouted, closing the gate. "I'll call you later, Donovan."

"You ready?" asked Donovan, holding the reins of Aunt Clare's old gelding horse.

"I hope this works," said Ben. "Are you sure about this horse?"

"Ol' Plug? Sure, he has three legs in the grave." Donovan adjusted the stirrup.

"It's the fourth one I'm worried about," replied Ben, nervously poised in his A.S.S. costume.

"Know what you're going to say?"

Ben nodded and trepidatiously nudged Plug through the gate of the boarding house, around the corner, to just beneath Ilyeana's third-floor window.

"Ilyeana," he called softly, unsure how Plug would react to loud noises.

"Louder," urged Donovan, standing out of sight.

Finally, Ben shouted her name. He saw Aunt Clare look out the parlor window, shake her head, and close the curtains. Then Ilyeana looked down from her window. Ben steadied the horse.

"'Tis I, your prince. My love for you burns brighter than all the stars," he proclaimed, before reciting a love sonnet Donovan had given him to memorize for the occasion.

"Wait! I come down," screeched Ilyeana from the open window. She bounded from her room, hitting the last step on a dead run. Aunt Clare smiled and opened the front door as Ilyeana streaked past her.

"I knew you were a prince," cooed Ilyeana all the way down the walk.

Plug whinnied and jerked sideways. Ilyeana reached up and plucked Ben from the stirrups. She removed his helmet and began kissing his face, cradling him in her arms.

"Seeing is believing," said Aunt Clare to Donovan, as he closed the front door.

Ben and Ilyeana's wedding was held the following week in the garden in the back of Aunt Clare's house. One day near the end of summer, while walking in the woods, Donovan saw Ben and Ilyeana in the grove of trees that surrounded their house. A carpet of fallen leaves and pine needles muffled his steps as he approached. Although Donovan was too far away to make out what they were saying, he heard their playful screams and joyous laughter echo among the trees.

Ben wielded his sword as he sat high upon Ilyeana's wide shoulders. Their metallic gray shapes darted among the trees. They laughed when Ilyeana suddenly slipped and fell on the damp, waxy needles beneath a large tree. In an instant, Ben was reseated. Ilyeana yelled something in Russian, Ben adjusted his helmet, tugged at his armor, and flailed at the lower branches of the tree as if they were Visigoth heads. Donovan smiled and turned quietly away.

Fröst

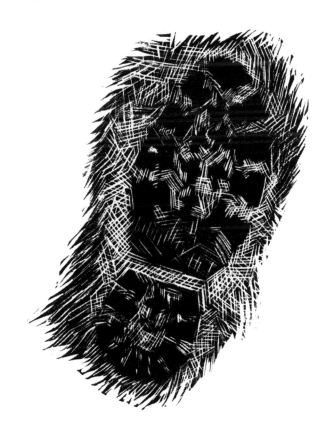

"You let me worry about that!" barked Bill Travis to Donovan with a chilling stare.

No one seemed to know what exactly happened after that winter day, but Donovan had done everything but get down on his knees and beg Bill to stop fooling around with Indian Bob's wife, Patti Feather, who pulled the sheets down for a lot of men in Allegory Falls. Donovan and Indian Bob were close friends, but so were he and Patti.

"Forget it, Donovan. He won't listen," said Itty McNeal, watching Bill go back to the pool table where he was losing his weekly unemployment check.

"I know. I wish it were that simple, though," replied Donovan. "We've known about Patti for some time. Whenever Bob goes out of town for a construction job, Patti latches onto the first man she sees. If it wasn't Bill, it'd be someone else. It's Bob I'm most concerned about."

"Yeah," replied Itty, looking at Donovan's troubled face. "Can you imagine what would happen if Bob found out it was Bill? Seems all we can do is just be the best friends we can be....We can't live their lives for them."

Bob Feather was part Crow, part Blackfoot and the rest English. Donovan pinned his nickname on him in grade school after Bob showed up at a Halloween party in full headdress and war paint. He scared everyone that night when, after Bill insulted his heritage, he drew that hunting knife and backed Bill into a corner. Bob liked the nickname–said it distinguished the better half of his ancestry. He was a handsome man with chocolate eyes, black hair and a neatly trimmed goatee that made him look more ominous than he was.

Donovan leaned against the bar. "Remember when we first met Bob? We were playing baseball in that gravel pit on your dad's ranch when Bob seemed to appear from nowhere."

"If I remember right, Bill was there too and didn't want Bob to play because he was Indian," replied Itty.

"Bill's nose has never been the same."

Donovan and Itty chuckled about how their friend John McGunnigan convinced Bill that day that Bob was going to play.

"It's true what they say, some things change and some things remain the same," said Itty.

"Patti changed. She was just a skinny, knock-kneed girl then, but she could hit, pitch and throw as well as anyone. To think how our lives have been so intertwined," sighed Donovan.

Patti Feather was now a slender, voluptuous woman with long blonde hair that hung midway on her bottom. She could turn a man's head faster than Donovan could turn a twist-top cap off a beer bottle.

"From freckles to false eyelashes," coldly replied McNeal. "You can't blame yourself."

"Bob and Patti asked me to write their wedding vows, remember?"

"You have a way with words, and they were beautiful words. You almost had McGunnigan crying that day."

"I have to do something."

McNeal pushed his glass toward Donovan. "Like I said, you can't blame yourself. It goes back to that stuff about things changing and being the same. Patti changed but they are still our friends. If you go mucking around, you risk losing both friendships. Besides, Indian Bob's gotta know what's going on, don't you think?"

Donovan stood with his arms folded, leaning against the back of the bar. "I don't know what to think anymore. Maybe Bill is right, it's none of our business."

"I sure smell trouble coming," replied Itty.

Donovan filled Itty's glass and handed it to him. "Aunt Clare always said, if you go looking for trouble, it won't go half as far looking for you."

"Bob should be coming home soon," Itty said.

"I know," replied Donovan, painfully. "It's no wonder he doesn't suspect anything. You ever notice that she never lets him out of her sight when he's home?"

"You'd think that mushy, lovey-dovey act she puts on would tip him off to something," replied McNeal.

"I've lost all respect for her," muttered Donovan.

"What respect?" snapped Itty. "She uses a barstool like a trapper uses a bear trap."

"Remember the time we all went swimming when we were twelve or thirteen?"

"Toadcock Flats. Sure, I remember. We all skinny-dipped, you, me, Bob and Patti," said Itty, leaning on the bar and resting his cheek against his hand. "We should have known something was different about Patti, right then and there."

Donovan scowled. "That was innocent enough. I was thinking about the pact we made that day. You know, when we swore we'd be friends forever."

"Cutting our fingers and pressing blood together so we'd be blood-brothers and sisters." Itty laughed and showed Donovan the faint scar on his index finger. "Whose idea was that anyway?"

"Bob's," they both answered.

"Well, speak of the devil," said McNeal.

Patti strolled through the door and perched next to Itty, turning slightly to glance quickly across the room at Bill.

"What can you possibly see in *him*?" grumbled Donovan, tilting his head toward Bill.

"You don't know what I need or what I see in anyone," said Patti. She crossed her legs, exposing plenty of thigh below her tight black skirt. She looked at McNeal. "You, too?"

"Donovan's right. We're concerned about you and Bob," said Itty.

"Who's going to tell him? You? Or you?" snapped Patti. "Neither of you could tell him, and neither could anyone else in this miserable little town."

"So if the problem is this town, why not live on the road with Bob?" said Donovan.

"Yeah, right. Me in a fifth-wheel trailer, living alongside a construction site," laughed Patti. "I need to feel alive, not lie around watching soaps with my hair in curlers all day."

Itty gently put his hand on her shoulder. "Why not end it, then? There'd be a lot less pain in the long run for you and Bob."

She pushed Itty's hand away. "We've been over that. No one's going to tell Bob. He wouldn't believe it anyway."

"I don't understand. All of us have been friends for such a long time—we've laughed together, cried together, even howled at the moon together," said Donovan, looking into her eyes. "We've loved you like a sister and Bob like a brother. What happened?"

"I grew up," she retorted, twisting off the stool. "You two are still stuck in the past somewhere."

"You call what you do, grown up?"

"Go to hell, you two." Patti turned with her drink in hand and walked toward the jukebox. "Let's get out of here," she whispered to Bill, kissing him on the cheek knowing Donovan and Itty were watching.

"What the hell she sees in him..." Itty said to Donovan as they watched them disappear into the night.

———

The brass bell above the door jangled. Heavy footsteps crossed the floor to the bar.

"We're not open," shouted Donovan, crouched behind the counter changing out a keg.

"You should lock your doors, then," rang a familiar voice.

"That you, Bob?" asked Donovan, lifting himself up slowly.

"It's me," replied Indian Bob.

"Thought you were in Nevada working on a new highway." Donovan stuck out his hand toward Bob. "Geezus, Bob," he snapped, staring at a piece of frost-covered sod Indian Bob threw onto the bar, "is this any way to greet an old friend?"

"Finished early." Bob frowned. "Found this boot print outside my bedroom window this morning."

"Geez, Bob," moaned Donovan. "Couldn't it have been

someone checking the power meter?"

"Exiting the window? On a Sunday?" replied Bob, taking a stool off the bar. "Patti doesn't know how it got there either, the lying bitch. People forget how footprints on frosted grass leave a pretty accurate impression."

Donovan was at a loss for words. "Are you okay, Bob?"

"Okay? You ask if I'm okay when my wife has been sleeping around? I feel just like that chunk of sod—cold and black."

Donovan handed Indian Bob a towel. "Here, clean off your hands and I'll get you a cup of coffee…and wipe the bar, too!"

"Make it a shot and a beer," groaned Bob. "The grass stays until the frost melts."

"C'mon, Bob…"

"Just bring the damn drinks," Bob snarled, even though he hardly ever drank. "And quit pretending you didn't know what was going on."

"Okay, but just this one," Donovan signed.

Bob guzzled the shot and beer. "So, who is it? And don't play your fancy word games with me, like you used to when we were kids."

"What good is telling you going to do?" asked Donovan.

"I have to know!" shouted Indian Bob.

Donovan sensed the emotions coiling and uncoiling within Bob as he tried to remain calm.

"Who?" Bob slammed his fists on the bar. "Tell me who belongs to this boot print!"

Donovan imagined Bob's bear-paw-sized hands around Bill and Patti's throats. He could not possibly begin to tell him about everyone who had slept with Patti.

"And if I do?" asked Donovan. "You promise—"

Indian Bob cut him off. "Hey, I'm not crazy. I just want to scare the bastard away," Bob said calmly, pushing his empty glasses toward Donovan. "I still love her, you know that…I'd do the same for you if you were in my shoes."

Donovan thought while Indian Bob finished another drink.

"Yeah, I know you would. Maybe she's not happy with you any-more, Bob. Patti may still love you, but just not that way. Maybe it's time for the both of you to move on," said Donovan, pained with each word he spoke.

"I know I haven't been home much in the last two years, but that's no reason to do what she's done," replied Bob. "But if it's time for us to split up, I'll let her make that choice. I want to hear her say it though."

Donovan remembered how Bob struggled his junior year in high school just to muster enough courage to ask Patti out on a real date, without McNeal and Donovan tagging along as they had since grade school. He knew Bob wouldn't give up on her that easily.

Donovan looked into Bob's woe-ful eyes. "Okay. It's Bill Travis…I'm sorry, Bob, really…I love the both of you…what could I do?"

Indian Bob stared at Donovan. It was as cold and chilling as the boot-stained evidence thawing on the bar between them.

"Thanks," Bob said quietly. He stood up and grabbed the piece of sod in hand. "I'll use this to make sure, though. Good to see you again, Donovan. And hey—you're still the best friend I'll ever have."

"Go easy," replied Donovan. He slumped against the bar and watched Bob disappear into the frosty, foggy air of a late fall morning.

"Did you hear about Bill and Patti running off together?" asked

McNeal when he had ordered a beer. "That doesn't sound right at all."

"Bob said he let her make the decision," answered Donovan.

"That's what I heard, too." McNeal gave Donovan a puzzled look. "I saw Bob working on that construction project on the old highway outside of town."

"I told him he should take the job so he could be close to Patti. I thought it would make a difference...evidently it didn't," answered Donovan, handing McNeal his beer.

"So where did they go? Bill didn't have any money."

Donovan shook his head. "Bob said he gave Patti a few

thousand dollars and the Camaro when she said she was leaving. You were right about things changing!"

"Yeah," murmured McNeal. "Kind of dead in here without Patti."

"I know. Let's bury it for now. How about a game of pool?"

"Sure."

Donovan laid his apron at the end of the bar where Patti always sat and walked to the table.

———

That evening Donovan sat slumped in his truck, having slowed for the construction zone where Bob was poised atop his earth-mover. Donovan contemplated the distinct possibility of having just passed over the remains of Bill and Patti. Speculating on the irony of how frequently Patti had run over Bob, he wondered if it was now Bob's turn. In time, after decades of frost heave, just possibly the remains of Bill and Patti might be discovered, but by then Indian Bob and the rest would be in the ground, too. "Nah," Donovan muttered, double-clutching his old truck and creeping past the fresh mounds of black soil.

Spring
Fëvër

 Aunt Clare stood at the doorway leading to the cellar, where Donovan was busy arranging and organizing boxes of odds and ends for Aunt Clare's annual spring yard sale.

"You've been down there all morning. I hope you're getting some work done and not just wasting time. I need you to run an errand for me soon," she hollered. Her voice deadened in the pungent air that smelled of freshly dug potatoes and burlap.

Donovan did not answer. He had just pulled a box off a top shelf from which his old mitt and a tattered baseball fell to the earthen floor. The plop of the ball hitting the dusty floor brought a flood of childhood memories. It had been years since he stood on the mound at the county field. He picked up the ball, shook the dust from the mitt and tucked it firmly under his arm. Then he started rubbing the ball between his hands and fingers to get the feel of the stitches once again. Looking across the cellar, he took dead aim at the potato sacks. With a methodical wind-up and snap of the arm, his fast ball thwopped into the old sacks, raising a whiff of dust as if they were a well-worn catcher's mitt. Donovan softly whispered, "Tom."

One spring season in Donovan's youth, the entire Allegory Falls Horned Frogs baseball team went to see *The Pride of the Yankees* at the Starlite Drive-in. Coach Perkins loaded the team in the back of his Chevy pickup truck after they won the county championship. Everyone got a little sick, the result of too many sodas, hot dogs, popcorn and Black Crows candy, but Tom Boyle fared the worst—he developed ALS that night. By the following season, Tom had made a miraculous recovery though, and showed no signs of the usually fatal disease. But everyone, including Coach Perkins, could not believe that Tom still had not learned the fundamentals of baseball after seven years. Perkins always threw his cap on the ground and screamed, "Jesus, Mary and Joseph, you couldn't hit a hanging curve ball if the Pope blessed your bat, Boyle." Tom would put on a long face and Perkins would eventually console him by asking, "What is it this time, Boyle?"

Aside from suffering normal childhood diseases such as chicken pox, measles, which he had contracted on three occasions, and the mumps, twice, Tom suffered numberless other ailments by the time he was twenty. After high school, he got a job as a projectionist, which added to his problems—whatever affliction was acted out on the big screen, Tom usually contracted it. The list was unbelievable. Once, after watching B*en Hur* at the Moxie Theater, he got leprosy; another time it was a rare tropical disease no one could pronounce except Doc Nichols, after watching T*he African Queen* and *Tarzan* at a Saturday double-feature matinee. After watching L*ove Story,* Tom baffled the medical world with a rare form of cancer. By this time, no one paid much attention to Tom's complaints.

Not surprisingly, Tom was Aunt Clare's best client. When he wasn't being poked, prodded, gagged and x-rayed by Doc Nichols, who seemed bemused by Tom's bi-weekly visits, he usually sat on the back porch of the boarding house, rocking in the water-damaged wicker chair, while Aunt Clare smelled up the kitchen cooking one of her homemade concoctions on the wood cook stove.

"Take this over to the Boyle place." Aunt Clare handed Donovan a paper sack. "Tom has definitely caught something this time. His voice sounded terrible the way it crackled and rattled. I don't believe I've ever heard him so under the weather."

"It's probably the phone. The storm last night left a lot of ice on the lines," replied Donovan, lacing his boots. "So, tell me, what's Tom have now, a new strain of flu or—"

"He said he's hot, sweaty and can't leave the house," interrupted Aunt Clare, who looked quite concerned. "You know, this time Tom might actually be sick."

"Sure. What placebo are you giving him—salted lard or sulphur tar?" Donovan asked, buttoning his coat.

"Neither. My special fever reducer and aromatic balm. You should know by now I never waste good medicine on someone who's feigning," replied Aunt Clare stodgily.

"But how do you know he isn't feigning again?"

"I can tell, dear," said Aunt Clare. Donovan made his way down the icy walk, closed the gate behind him and disappeared into the snowy veil.

Tom's two-story house, draped in pillowy layers of snow, sat in a

clearing at the end of Cloot's Lane guarded by ash, birch and linden trees. Donovan wedged his way into the basement of the house through a narrow, rectangular crawl space in the stone foundation. It was coated with several inches of rust-colored ice.

Donovan skated carefully across the icy basement, where a good two and a half feet of ice covered the floor, and up the steps to the kitchen, where Tom greeted him. Tom's eyes were glassy and red, as if he hadn't slept in a month. Steam rose from his angular body while he paced back and forth between the counter and the dinette table in his Fruit of the Looms. From his rimpled brow, beads of sweat fell to the floor and quickly froze.

"You look like hell," Donovan said, handing Tom the paper bag. "Have you tried sleeping?"

"In my condition? If I lay down, I'd probably drown," said Tom.

Donovan slipped and caught hold of the table just as his legs began to go out from under him. "Do you want me to get Doc Nichols?"

"No point. He's already given me every possible test. He said he'd never seen anything like it and there was nothing he could do for me medically." Tom stopped to read Aunt Clare's instructions. Donovan tried to uproot a chair from the bed of ice carpeting the kitchen's red and white checked linoleum.

"You're wasting your time—they're frozen to the floor," muttered Tom, rubbing the red balm across his chest. "You'll have to stand, or sit on the table."

"What's with all this ice? The place is a disaster," said Donovan, sitting on the tabletop. He looked down and saw the remnants of Tom's last supper. A heavy layer of ice covered the plate and utensils like the clear polyurethane resin used to encase priceless memorabilia. A knife and fork lay on the plate like the hands of a clock that had stopped.

"I got so damn hot, I had to turn off the heat and open the windows. Before I could get the water shut off, the pipes burst, and now the heat from my body is causing all this condensation."

Donovan shivered as he stared into the living room. The stairs were a frozen waterfall and the rest of the house was a cavern of icy blue stalactites and stalagmites. He fastened the top button of his coat.

"It's five degrees outside! You must have a hypothalamic disorder."

Tom looked at Donovan like he did not appreciate the news about the temperature. "Not really. It's more complicated than that."

"Then what is it?"

"I'm not sure. It all began about five weeks ago, after I went to a conference of the American Association of Movie

Projectionists in L.A.," began Tom. "It was a Sunday morning and I was cruising down a boulevard about to leave town when I noticed cars pulling into a drive-in that looked just like the Starlite."

Donovan knew Tom could not pass up a chance to see a movie. "You aren't making any sense. What's this have to do with—"

"I'm getting to that," said Tom, pausing to unwrap a candy bar Aunt Clare had included in her package. It popped and crackled between his teeth like a broken window. "I figured what the heck, people in California do things differently, maybe they showed movies on Sunday mornings. It did seem strange that there was no attendant and only a sign above a padlocked kettle that read: A Two Dollar Donation Is Appreciated. I went in, set the speaker on the window and the next thing I knew, I was part of a church service. This guy, Sonny Arkis, came on the screen. He was wearing a jade sharkskin suit with a peach-colored tie. His face looked like a gravel road, and he had the biggest, whitest teeth I've ever seen. He shouted, 'Welcome to the Church of the Redeemed and Anointed Pentecostals of Latter-day Apostles.' You familiar with his radio and TV shows? They're very popular."

C.R.A.P.O.L.A., Donovan thought to himself with amusement. "Uh, no. I'm Catholic, remember?"

"Oh, yeah," said Tom. "Arkis is a faith healer, you know, so when he got to the point in the service of praying over people, he asked the people in the cars to pray along."

"Big deal—you attended a funky church service. What's that got to do with all this?" Donovan gestured to the frozen floor.

"I'm getting to that, if you give me a chance. I was just about to put the speaker back on the post, when Arkis started getting all worked up. He said there was someone present who needed deliverance from a life of affliction and disease. As sick as I've been over the years, I thought he meant me, so I listened intently while he chastised the devil and went on about giving your heart to Jesus, and surrendering to the cleansing fire of God." Tom

reached over and broke an icicle off the cupboard. He slowly rubbed it on his forehead. "I didn't care so much about the other stuff as just getting healed."

"You were actually expecting a miracle?"

"Sure, I guess," replied Tom, bluntly. "I touched the speaker box, like he said, while he prayed. I figured it couldn't hurt, stranger things have happened. They had ushers who walked around, prayed with you, gave you a brochure, and asked for another donation. One came and prayed over me."

"And you thought you would be cured?"

"You know how hard it is to be sick all the time?" asked Tom, plaintively.

Donovan winced.

"After I got home, I started watching Arkis's TV show. When I didn't feel well, I touched the screen while he prayed."

Donovan tried to picture Tom kneeling next to his TV, which sat beneath a movie poster for *Harvey*, holding one hand to the screen, which was now coated with milky ice. He wondered if Tom reached his other hand toward heaven, like he used to in left field. And like then, Donovan thought sadly, Tom missed the ball.

"The last time I held my hand to the TV, I think I did start to feel warm and tingly all over. The more I touched the screen, the hotter I became. At first, it felt good...I thought I was finally receiving the miracle Arkis raved about. But all that day, I kept getting hotter and hotter. I knew right away I had contracted something really severe. You can see what happened," said Tom, leaning against the counter.

"I need to get you some help!" Donovan stood up.

"Don't leave just yet," Tom pleaded. "I told you that I've been through every test. I tried calling Arkis himself but I got this pre-recorded message—for Salvation, Press 1; for Miracles, Press 2; for Prayer and Supplications, Press 3; for all others, Press 4. When I did, a woman with an angelic voice answered. She was very sym-pathetic, but couldn't help me, and referred me to 3. The person at Prayer and Supplication said I definitely needed a miracle and to Press 2. When I did, that person said first I had to be saved and to Press 1, but I told them that I just wanted to speak to Arkis."

"And what did Arkis say?"

"I never got to talk to him."

Donovan watched Tom pace back and forth. Wherever he stepped, his feet melted the ice, which froze again when he stepped away. The kitchen turned white as the sun crept through the sheets of ice that were once windows. Tom's body looked even hotter in the eerie glow.

"And you think Aunt Clare's medicine will actually help?"

"I hate to tell you this, but her medicine isn't working like it used to. Smells kinda good though." Tom paused. "Is it getting colder outside?"

"Yeah, supposed to be well below zero tonight," replied Donovan.

"And I'm on fire. Oh, well, things could be worse," Tom said, with a wry smile.

"How so?"

"It could be summer. You better go, it won't be long before that crawl space freezes over."

Tom walked with him to the basement door. As Donovan went carefully down the steps, it suddenly occurred to him that all Tom needed was to watch the right movie—maybe something like *Angels in the Outfield*.

"I have a great idea..." he hollered from the bottom of the stairs.

Tom smiled. "It's okay. Spring's not far off," he shouted.

———

When Donovan finally emerged from the cellar, Aunt Clare scolded him. "At last! The grocery store is going to close soon. What took you so long down there anyway? I could have done it faster myself!" she said, shaking her head.

"Reminiscing," said Donovan, setting a large box of yard-sale items by the back door, among them his old glove, ball and a Nellie Fox Model Louisville Slugger.

Things did get worse for Tom. Spring had come early and with it a rapid thaw. Youngsters of all ages were slapping their mitts and honing their skills on the diamond. Coach Perkins was still yelling at players who, like Tom, couldn't catch, throw, or swing a bat.

But none of it had the thrill it once held for Donovan. On opening day, Donovan went to Legion Field and scattered Tom's ashes around home plate. After a short eulogy by the coach, the umpire swept off the plate, donned his mask, and yelled, "Play ball!"

dust
dëvils

 "He still owes a week's rent," grumbled Aunt Clare as she and Sandy pulled the sheets off the bed. "Just look at this stain…didn't he ever wash his hair? Better throw it away and get a new one, dear," sighed Aunt Clare, handing the pillowslip to her niece.

"I wonder what really became of him." Sandy wadded the soiled linen into a ball and tossed it in the laundry basket. "I heard he hooked up with some criminals."

"Nonsense," Aunt Clare said, closing the door. "There's nothing of the like around here. Who knows what young people think today—they're as flighty as the wind."

Leonard Tuttle, the new mechanic at Prescott's Texaco, had black hair that hung straight from the weight of hair tonic, thick glasses, and a slouching shuffle. He was happiest covered with oil and grease and working on a good V-8. He rolled back in the desk chair behind the grease-stained oak desk, stretched and watched a dust devil spin across the highway. He sat mesmerized while the twisting vortex spat dirt and trash, moving toward the gas station with increasing speed. A cold spasm jerked Leonard's spine when the spinning mass pelted the window and blew through the screen door, scattering the papers on the desk. Leonard recalled what his mother had told him as a child. "Never stand in the path of a dust devil. It's the devil's way of taking your soul from you." Although Leonard never believed her, he now unconsciously quivered in the chair. He rubbed his eyes, smearing black ninety-weight oil on his cheeks. A dark, glossy Lincoln Continental eased up to the pumps and the driver jogged to the pay phone.

"We're getting closer, boss," a gritty-throated Frank Rich said into the pay phone outside the station while Louie Card refueled their sleek, gun-metal gray Lincoln with suicide doors. "We should have the problem disposed of in a day or so."

"Hey, kid," Louie shouted to Tuttle, leaning his head out the passenger window. "Yeah, you. You ever seen this guy hanging around these parts?" He pulled a crumpled three-by-five photo from his suit coat and sharply snapped the picture at Leonard, who had approached the car.

"Mmmm…I dunno," Leonard sheepishly replied. He held the photo closer and contorted his face. "Looks kind of familiar, but I don't think so."

"Take another frigging look," grumbled Frank as he made his way through the opening between the two gas pumps. "A real close look this time."

"He looks like a lot of people…I guess he could be here," replied Leonard, with Frank peering over his shoulder.

"Look kid," snapped Louie. "You see a lot of people come and go here, right? So all we're asking is that you take a good look and tell us if you've seen a guy that looks like this. Either you did or you didn't."

Leonard darted his eyes back and forth from Louie to Frank. "I haven't seen a lot of people—I've only worked here a couple of weeks, so I can't really say for sure." He shakily handed the photo back to Louie.

"Yeah, can't say or won't say," barked Louie.

"Honest, if I could help you, sir, I would."

"Aw, leave the kid alone." Frank opened the door and climbed behind the wheel. "He's too stupid to know anything."

Louie handed a twenty to Leonard. "Well, if you see anybody that looks vaguely like that picture, you let us know right away, got it?"

"We're staying at the Cloud 9 Motel, Room 7," said Frank. "Might be something more in it for you, if you help us out." He flashed Leonard a wink as he gunned the engine and sped off down the highway.

A whirling gray cloud of exhaust and dust swallowed Leonard. He walked back to the office, pocketing the money.

"So, how'd your day go?" asked Donovan when Leonard came into Haig's Bar that night. He slid a pint toward Leonard, who promptly sat himself on a stool.

"OK. Thanks again for helping me get that job," Leonard answered. He took a deep breath and hesitated. Then he said, "There were these two guys, though...they looked like—"

"Like those two?" interrupted Donovan, motioning to the back of the room where Louie and Frank sat at the far corner table.

"That's them," whispered Leonard, staring at them briefly. He pulled the glass to his lips.

"They've been here about an hour or so," Donovan said, tossing the bar towel over his shoulder. "Asked a lot of questions and showed a photograph of somebody no one's ever seen before."

"Exactly. Do they look normal to you?" Leonard asked, discreetly peering over his shoulder through the dim light of the bar to where Frank and Louie sat with their backs turned. Leonard didn't have to see the black-as-night, recessed eyes in Louie's oversized head to feel a chill rush over him, nor did he have to see Frank's long, narrow face shaped like a vise, or the thick, pink scar that zigzagged above the cleft in his chin to know that these were the two who had intimidated him. He fidgeted with his glass. "So, who do you think they are?"

"Who knows?" replied Donovan, washing the glasses in the sink below the bar. "Badly dressed mobsters? Maybe they're looking for someone who ratted on their boss," he added, chuckling.

"Allegory Falls would be the perfect place for witness relocation, it's so isolated."

"Oh, right. Undoubtedly." Donovan dried his hands and laughed. "Are you listening to yourself there, Leonard?"

"Well, it's possible."

"You've watched too many movies," Donovan said, moving to the other end of the bar.

Suddenly, Louie's hand dug into Leonard's shoulder. "Remember what we said, kid," he whispered, bending over Leonard's shoulder. "If you know something, you better come pay us a visit."

Frank winked at him again, and he and Louie left, their patent leather loafers clicking across Haig's wooden floor. "That kid knows something," Louie muttered to Frank. "I just know it."

Leonard finished his beer deep in thought and left the bar. Maybe there was something in it for him, he thought, strolling along the highway to the edge of town, where the flashing yellow and orange sign for the Cloud 9 Motel pierced the heavy night sky.

Leonard stood outside the motel room, nervously scratching the concrete step with his foot. He raised his hand slowly to the door, where the tarnished brass 7 hung slightly askew. The dull yellow entrance light made his hand look like a ripe pear. He took a deep breath and knocked.

"Yeah?" barked Frank, reaching across his body to unholster a stubby pistol from a worn leather holster. "Who is it?"

"Leonard."

"Leonard who?" Frank got up off the bed and moved toward the door, cocking his pistol.

"Leonard Tuttle. I work at the gas station, remember?" He quickly tugged the lapels and ends of his coat when he heard the latch turn.

"Whadaya want?" Frank lashed, putting his pistol away, and opening the door an eye's width.

"Who's there?" asked Louie, stepping from the bathroom and reaching for his 9 mm automatic on the nightstand.

"Cool it," Frank said. "It's just that kid from the gas station."

"Well, get him in here before someone sees him," snapped Louie.

Frank opened the door wider, grabbed Leonard by the shoulder and yanked him into the room. "Get in here and tell us something we don't already know," he said, shoving Leonard into a chair next to the door.

"I do know someone who stands out from the rest of the locals and…"

"You could have said that earlier and saved us some time, dammit," snarled Louie, scratching himself.

"So, does anybody know you're here?"

"No," Leonard replied, swallowing hard.

"You'd better not be lying this time."

Leonard's eyes grew big. "Honest, no one knows I'm here."

"OK, kid," sighed Frank, "we believe you. Just tell us what you know, so we can get you that reward we promised."

"You guys aren't cops, are you?" asked Leonard, pivoting his head back and forth between Louie and Frank.

"Well, aren't you clever," sneered Frank. Light from the lamp glittered in his dark eyes.

"Let's cut to the chase, kid," barked Louie, muscling Leonard up from the chair, close to his face. "Now start giving us some real answers. My patience is wearing thin with all this chit chat." He shoved Leonard back into the chair.

"Someone came into the station last week with a flat to repair. Gave me a five-dollar tip. He looks a little like the guy in the photo, but not exactly."

"How, not exactly?" asked Frank, blowing a puff of cigar smoke that swirled in the dim light above Leonard's head.

Leonard coughed. "The hair is different—shorter, and not as dark."

"Go on." Louie slid into his size 42 trousers.

"And he was wearing glasses and looked a little heavier." Leonard was gaining confidence with every detail he added.

"Now we're getting somewhere," replied Louie. "So, where is this person?"

"He said he lived on a couple of acres across the river," said Leonard, sensing a big payoff. "I can give you directions."

"Better yet, you can show us." Frank and Louie checked their weapons and put on their coats. Louie pulled Leonard to his feet.

"Here," he said, grabbing Leonard's hand. "Here's the keys—you're driving."

"But—"

"But nothing," said Louie. "Just get in the car."

"I think this is the place," said Leonard.

"Cut the lights," snapped Frank, leaning over the rear seat. Leonard slowed, nearing the lone house at the end of the narrow lane. "Pull up close to the back door real slow, and keep the engine running."

"Wait right here," Louie said when the car stopped. "And you better be here when we get back!"

Leonard slumped behind the wheel of the purring Lincoln in the darkness, watching Louie and Frank enter the house like they had lived there all their lives. He thought of Donovan saying he watched too many movies—this wasn't like anything he'd seen. He pressed his hand on the door latch until he heard the release mechanism click. Just as he was about to open the door and run, he heard them coming back.

"Open the trunk!" spit Louie urgently.

Leonard momentarily froze in place as Frank and Louie made their way down the back steps carrying a bundle wrapped in a patchwork comforter, with two bare feet sticking out.

"Open the trunk," Frank bellowed again. "You frigging deaf?"

"I told you not to get anyone involved again," huffed Louie. "Can't we do a job without—"

"Shut...up," Frank hissed. "No need scaring the kid."

They waited while Leonard fumbled with the keys.

"It's the round one, you idiot," growled Frank. "Haven't you ever unlocked a trunk before?"

When the trunk popped open, Louie and Frank gave the roll a hefty toss. It landed with a dull thunk.

"Is he...?" asked Leonard, nervously.

"Now, what do you think?" wheezed Frank. Louie slammed the trunk lid and the neighbor's dog started barking.

"Let's get out of here," Louie said.

"But, w-wait a minute..." stammered Leonard.

"Wait nothing! Just get in and drive," snarled Frank, sliding into the back seat.

Leonard steered the Lincoln onto the highway and gathered speed. "So, I get my reward, right?" he said with forced cheerfulness.

"Sure, kid," replied Frank. "We never go back on our word."

"Back to the motel?" Leonard assumed a confident posture behind the wheel.

"Are you kidding?" laughed Louie. "Head south, and quit asking so many questions, will you?"

"But I have to open the station at 6 a.m."

Frank moved forward and put his cold hand on Leonard's shoulder. "We have to take care of loose ends first." He paused. "I think your days working at that piss-poor excuse for a gas station are over." Louie turned to look back at Frank, the folds of his frown turning white.

Leonard stared out at the highway and thought back on all the gangster movies he had seen. He was a dead man. The mob never let anyone who knew too much live.

"The boss is buying us a Cadillac after we finish this job," Frank said to Louie. "I was thinking we should get us a driver." He nodded toward the kid.

"Looks like you're driving from now on," grumbled Louie. "I bet you thought you were going to end up like that stiff in the trunk," he added, laughing.

Leonard looked in the rearview mirror. Frank was smiling. Leonard thought for a moment, relaxed his deathgrip on the steering wheel, and grinned. He hoped the Cadillac was a Fleetwood with a 429 cubic inch V-8. He pressed down on the accelerator, and the car roared down the highway, humming across the fissures in the asphalt as the newly painted median lines sped like flashing bullets in the burgeoning glow of a reddening horizon.

Someday, Seurat

 "But, Aunt Clare, it's only for a little while, until he can find another place," Donovan pleaded.

"You know my policy," she replied, busily pinning pieces of another quilt. "Besides, the last time someone said it was only for a little while was over thirty years ago, when your cousin Halbert showed up on the doorstep."

"I think he made up that part about being related, Aunt Clare."

"Well, it's too late to do anything about that now," she replied.

"Seurat is not like...your average—"

"Dog, Donovan," interrupted Aunt Clare. "He's a dog. And what kind of name is Sir-rat, anyway?"

"Seurat," corrected Donovan. "It's French. He's named after an artist."

"French or not, I can't have a dog in the house."

Aunt Clare was sure that a dog would disturb her cat, Abdullah's, gentle disposition. The tomcat was ratty as shag carpet that had never been cleaned, with scars where his whiskers used to be, and he strutted around the house gurgling and ruffling his hair at everyone. She was nonetheless convinced that Abdullah was gentle.

"But they'll freeze to death," insisted Donovan. "The county couldn't find a place for them." Malsch had been evicted by the county health department from the abandoned bunkhouse that was once used by the Union Pacific Railroad before the train quit running to Allegory Falls. Donovan knew Aunt Clare had a soft spot for the less fortunate.

"Well, if it will make you quit hounding me, then, okay," she replied. "Just mind that dog."

With Donovan's help, Malsch and Seurat moved into a room on the third floor in the rear of the house. Aunt Clare had wanted the dog the furthermost point away from her beloved cat, and the seclusion seemed appropriate for the disparate artist and his mottled companion.

Malsch had blue eyes and fine features that were framed by sandy, mop-string hair that hovered just above his shoulders and hid his oily, frayed collars. His gaunt face was covered with a number of small brown moles and sparse blonde stubble, and he smelled of poverty, turpentine and dog.

Seurat was a dumpy, bowlegged bull terrier, well past the age of running amok but he was, nonetheless, attached to a worn cotton rope that more often than not trailed between the dog's fleshy, pink haunches that were also covered with brown moles and sparse hairs.

"You were right," said Aunt Clare as she and Donovan made their way down the stairs from Malsch's room. "Did you see the way they were shivering? Is Malsch his first name or last?"

"I don't know," said Donovan. "I think it's both."

"A dog with a French name and a man with only one name." A befuddled look folded over Aunt Clare's face. "Who has just one name?"

"He's an artist. Artists are a different breed."

"I know art, and what he does doesn't look like art to me," said Aunt Clare.

Until Aunt Clare visited his room, only Donovan had known that Malsch painted anything more than storefront signs and barroom murals.

"There's all types of art. He's a modern artist."

"Well, modern or not, the poor man just won't survive on those things," replied Aunt Clare. "No one wants to look at people with three eyes, blue hair and orange lips."

"It's called cubism," said Donovan patiently. "But that's only a part of his work…there's surrealism, abstraction, and—"

"Never mind, dear," interrupted Aunt Clare. "It will never replace a good painting of flowers."

"Or a cat?" needled Donovan.

"That too, dear."

"What can I get you?" Donovan asked. Malsch and Seurat had just hobbled into Haig's Bar. Their arthritic gaits and forlorn looks announced the persistence of winter.

"Maybe you'd like a small mural painted," said Malsch, taking a seat at the bar.

"Why do you waste your talent on that?" asked Donovan, fixing Malsch a cup of hot buttered rum. "If you need the money, I can lend you some."

"Thanks, but you and your aunt have been kind enough already." Malsch shivered as he sipped his drink.

"I suppose you could use a portion of the back hallway," said Donovan hesitantly. "It's near the toilets, but that's the best I can do. Haig doesn't want much done to the place. Says it's unnecessary, since the people around here are accustomed to brass fixtures and stuffed heads."

"That's fine with me," replied Malsch. "A hundred okay?"

"I think I can swing that."

"Good, I'll get started right away."

Most bars in Allegory Falls have a Malsch, as they are known, usually a half-naked cowgirl atop a bucking horse sprawled across the wall. He once painted a scene of a naked woman blowing the chest cavity out of a bull elk with a hunting rifle, or at least it resembled an elk, in the Ponderosa Bar. It was hard to tell from the glazed eyes of the clientele what was more popular, the naked woman or the blood-splattering explosion.

"I prefer doing tropical scenes, you know." Malsch reached down for his paint case. "I keep telling Seurat, 'Titties and trees, that's all they know, but someday, Seurat, someday.'"

"I have a better idea," said Donovan. "Instead of a mural, just paint whatever you like and we'll hang it over the bar mirror."

"Good. I'll paint it in my room, if you don't mind," said Malsch. He motioned to Seurat with his head. "Let's go, we have work to do."

Seurat nibbled at Malsch's heels, begging to be carried. The old dog must have calculated that he was owed something for all the times he helped guide the staggering artist home.

"You can walk," groaned Malsch. "You have four, I have two."

———

Several days later, Donovan noticed Malsch's door was slightly ajar. He knocked softly and stuck his head through the opening.

"Mind if I come in?" he asked.

"I'm kind of busy but—"

"I understand. I was just curious how you were progressing with the painting."

"Come in," said Malsch. "I get so focused sometimes I forget my manners. Please, come in."

"I can come back later—I didn't mean to interrupt."

"No, do come in, I can use a break," replied Malsch, opening the door. "Sit down."

"Is that the painting?"

"Yes."

"I had no idea it was going to be so large," said Donovan, looking from the floor to the ceiling.

"You don't like it?"

"No, no. I do." Donovan cocked his head from side to side and moved around the room, looking at it from every angle. "Reminds me of Hopper, Van Gogh and Picasso all rolled into one."

"You seem to know a lot about art."

"I read a lot of books. Never studied art like you, though."

"Oh, I never studied art," replied Malsch. "I mean, I went to the college and all, but only for part of a semester. They wanted to talk more about art than make it, so I left."

"There you are," said Aunt Clare, sticking her head around the corner of the partially opened door. "I wanted you to bring this up to Mr. Malsch and save me the trip up those frightful stairs." She handed a quilt to Malsch. "This should keep you warmer."

Malsch hung his head shyly as he took the quilt from Aunt Clare and thanked her. The colors even matched Malsch's painting.

"Poor substitute for curtains," said Aunt Clare, scowling at the oiled paper Malsch used to cover up the windows. "I thought artists liked natural light?"

"I prefer subdued light. It makes the room turn butter-colored in the day," Malsch replied. Donovan knew Malsch was constantly dreaming of the tropical sun that looked like butterscotch at sun-rise.

"It's a good thing the room faces the back, otherwise the neighbors would think I've lost my mind." Aunt Clare stared at Seurat, who had his ears pinned back and looked guilty as a kid in a candy store.

"So, what do you think of Malsch's painting? He's doing it for the bar," said Donovan, trying to steer Aunt Clare away from Malsch's living habits.

"The color is nice…and…I'm sure…everyone will enjoy it." Aunt Clare paused. "Why are there so many naked bodies?"

"It's all I learned to paint in art school. I was only there a very short time," said Malsch.

You could almost hear Aunt Clare stop breathing. Maybe she was glad Malsch covered the windows with oiled paper.

"It's unfortunate that you never finished," replied Aunt Clare with a smile that Donovan had seen before when she tried not to hurt someone's feelings.

"Yes, perhaps," replied Malsch, "but I prefer my own approach to art."

"I can see that," Aunt Clare said hesitantly. "Have you seen my cat?" she added, looking at Seurat, who was eyeing a lump in the unfurled quilt on the bed.

"No," replied Malsch. "I want to thank you again for the quilt. It is beautiful. You are quite an artist in your own right."

Aunt Clare blushed. She knew she had a special gift when it came to quilts, even though Donovan doubted they possessed special powers. Donovan rolled his eyes as he got up off the gal-vanized milk can padded with a worn red velour pillow with gold tassles that Malsch used as a stool.

"Come now, Donovan," said Aunt Clare moving toward the door. "Help me find the cat."

"What's with the quilt?" Donovan asked her as they searched the lower floors for Abdullah. "You're up to something, I know it."

"Nonsense, dear," she replied. "I just couldn't bear to see that poor man shiver all the time."

But Donovan knew Aunt Clare did not give away her quilts without a purpose. He imagined Malsch and Seurat cuddled beneath it, twittering and twitching like puppies, dreaming of new horizons filled with butter-colored light, while Aunt Clare's magic went to work.

"I think I know why," said Donovan, quickly withdrawing a bloody hand from beneath the sofa. "I thought you only used the quilts for good?"

Aunt Clare stood smiling like she had just swallowed the proverbial canary when Abdullah came hissing and darting past them.

No one expected that Malsch would ever be more than a painter of signs and barroom nudes, but that changed the following spring.

While visiting her brother in Allegory Falls, Teal Ramos, the owner of a small gallery in New York, caught sight of Malsch's painting through the glass door of Haig's and took an instant liking to his style.

A tall, thin young woman, Teal wore her dark hair in a French braid so long she looked as if she might topple over any minute from the weight. Her turquoise eyes were accentuated by long, mesmerizing lashes. She was dressed in a black jumpsuit interlaced with silver threads that refracted light like a mirror ball. The low-cut suit exposed nearly as much as Malsch's murals and when she strolled across the wooden floor in her stiletto heels, silence befell the bar. After she left someone even claimed that the music in the jukebox actually stopped, but such was the case with the numb minds that frequented Haig's.

"You're serious?" asked Donovan, astounded and happy.

"Of course I am," Teal replied, in a nasal tone. "Is there some other reason that you can think of that would bring me through that door?"

"No, I wasn't implying any- thing," Donovan quickly answered. "I've just never heard anyone refer to Malsch as undiscovered talent before."

"This Malsch, does he live around here?" she asked.

"Yes, he lives in my aunt's boarding house."

"Does he paint anything other than these kitschy murals?" Teal asked, opening her small handbag and taking out a business card. "Or is his work confined to painting eroticism for the locals?"

"Actually, he paints other things…mostly modern…but he's rather secretive about his painting." Donovan was unsure how to explain Malsch's work to her. "I've only seen them briefly myself."

"Can you give me directions to your aunt's boarding house?" asked Teal.

"If you can wait until six, I'll drive you." Donovan mixed her a drink and made small talk. For two hours he developed a headache pretending he knew what she was talking about concerning art.

———

Seurat lay on the bed of blankets while Malsch sat, with a faint smile, watching Teal's reactions squirm across her body the way only art aficionados can react to modern art. She examined each of his canvasses carefully. Malsch was comforted by the way she kept repeating to herself, "Yes, yes, this works for me." The artsy words that followed escaped Malsch altogether. Seurat seemed to understand, by the way he continually cocked his head and wagged his tail.

"So post-modernist," Teal said, turning to Malsch, whose head was still abuzz with the way she kept repeating "Oh, Gawd, yes." All he could do was nod and smile agreeably.

She shook her head slowly, side to side. "Amazing that no one has discovered your work before now."

"This is Allegory Falls," said Donovan, who stood in the opposite corner watching her closely. "You can do something with these paintings?"

"Oh, Gawd yes," she replied. "I can do great things with them in New York."

Malsch listened to Teal explain how she would represent his work, and dreamed of a lemon-colored sun, the beach and turquoise water.

"Just keep painting," Teal assured Malsch. "The future abounds with promise." Malsch smiled and waved shyly as Teal drove away.

———

Malsch and Donovan spent the next several weeks crating his artwork exactly as Teal had instructed, with money she left as an advance. Once the paintings were hung in The Painted Planet in New York, Malsch settled back to his punctilious routine of painting by day and dreaming by night. He dreamt of Teal, warm weather and golden light. Much to the displeasure of Seurat, Malsch flinched and talked in his sleep, repeating, "Oh, Gawd, yes."

"You heard anything yet?" Donovan asked Malsch one day

while they sat on the front stoop.

"Just a letter now and then saying everything for the show is progressing nicely."

"Seems to me you should be happier than you appear to be."

"She wants me to fly to New York for the reception," said Malsch. "I remember those things from school. Just a lot of people smiling really shallow, then turning their backs to giggle, while they drink wine and eat cheese."

"A small price to pay for fame," said Donovan. "Say, who's your favorite artist?"

"Ike Sankey," Malsch said without any hesitation.

"Who's he?"

"My uncle."

"Painter?"

"No," replied Malsch. "Chainsaw sculptor. Cuts out bears, cowboys and the like from logs, then sells them in parking lots during tourist season. Makes enough money to live in Arizona every winter."

"Besides him, then," persisted Donovan.

"Gauguin," he replied softly. "He lived in Tahiti."

"Gauguin had to deal with galleries, too. And ended up, I guess, where he wanted to be. Just think of it that way," said Donovan. "Your day is coming." He stood up and patted Malsch on the shoulder.

———

"What's this?" asked Aunt Clare as she took a postcard from Donovan.

"It's from Malsch, to the both of us. He's living in Mexico with Teal," answered Donovan as he collapsed on the couch. "She sold his paintings and the gallery, too."

"No need reading it, dear, now that you have told me everything," she said, handing the card back to him. "It worked, it really worked." She clapped her hands.

"What worked?"

"The quilt, dear."

"The quilt? You think it actually had something to do with his success?"

"Well, the dog isn't here anymore now, is it?" she chirped. "Never made a quilt for a dog before, but it worked."

As Aunt Clare jubilantly went on about the power of her quilts, Donovan turned his thoughts to Malsch and Seurat. He could see them dance in the sand as a yellow light engulfed them. Their winter villa in Cabo San Lucas overlooking crystal blue waters was now home, even though they would return each summer to Allegory Falls for inspiration. After Teal made Malsch an international success and sold her gallery, the three have been inseparable.

The warmth of the Mexican sun finally reached into the dry, cold bones of Malsch and Seurat. Malsch traded his moth-eaten wool coat for a peasant shirt, shorts, Panama hat and hand-craft-ed leather sandals. Seurat's once lifeless gait now had bounce.

As for Teal and Malsch, well, they smiled at one another a lot. Malsch spent carefree hours in the local cantinas painting bright-ly colored tropical murals of half-naked women, who looked a lot like Teal, atop dancing bulls, much to the delight of the patrons. His dream had come true.

In the glow of the brilliant sunset after a day of painting, Malsch and Seurat made their way along the warm, wet sand toward the villa where Teal eagerly awaited them. Malsch looked down at the prancing Seurat and said, "See, I told you so. Someday, Seurat, someday."

The Writing Lesson

 Donovan Magruder always wanted to be a writer. He knew that from the moment he found his aunt Clare's Underwood typewriter gathering dust in the attic of Magruder's boarding house. From that day on, he spent every free moment banging away at the worn and sticky keys, and with an ample supply of paper and a can of 3-in-1 oil, he forged his stories. And given the character of Allegory Falls, there was never a shortage of ideas for the fledgling writer.

"You should enter this contest," said Itty McNeal soon after he took a stool at Haig's Bar, where Donovan worked. He pointed to the inside of an empty matchbook cover lying on the bar. "You're good at writing and telling stories, and there's a $250 cash prize."

Donovan took the matchbook from his friend and read the inside cover quickly. "First prize is writing lessons from an established author. Think of it! Me getting writing lessons from a well-known writer."

"Those things are bunk," inserted John McGunnigan. "My cousin entered one, the Draw-Me thing. You know, where you draw some goofy cartoon dog. Well, after awhile, this guy showed up on the doorstep with a $250 prize alright, but it was good only if he applied it to the whole course, which cost $795."

"And what happened?" asked Itty.

"He took the course because it promised a lucrative career in the arts." McGunnigan imitated the pitchman's tone. "Well, he finished it, didn't get any job, and now he's paying ten bucks a month plus interest to pay off the balance of the course."

"This is different. It's writing. And it says all prizes are guaranteed," replied Itty, tearing the cover off the matchbook and handing it to Donovan. "Give it a try. You can buy a lot of paper and ribbon with $250."

"And don't forget the personalized instruction from an established author," McGunnigan sneered. "Probably somebody who published his own book at a vanity press."

Donovan stared long at the matchbook. "Nothing to lose, I guess," he mumbled, tucking the match cover into his shirt pocket.

"I recognized you from the photo on the covers of your books. I really liked *The Coveting Chronicles*," said Donovan excitedly, as he carried Sanford Aster's steamer trunk up the narrow, wallpapered stairway to the third-floor room Aunt Clare reserved for guests.

Aster wheezed and stopped before reaching the landing. He took a silk handkerchief from the lapel pocket of his tweed jacket and wiped his brow. "Why, thank you, son."

"Are you alright, Mr. Aster?" Donovan stood on the landing looking down the steep incline with the trunk perched on his shoulder.

"I'm fine, just a little out of shape. You go ahead. I'll catch up." Aster was a rotund man, in his seventies, with thick, bristly white hair, round, black glasses and a pencil moustache. "If I don't die first," he mumbled to himself.

"I'm really excited about having the opportunity to work with someone of your caliber." Donovan led Aster to the room. "I expected someone I had never heard of. Honestly, I am overwhelmed. But I must confess I thought you were dead."

"Why's that, young man?" Aster cocked his head and stuck out his jaw.

"Your last novel was written over...over...," Donovan drew a blank.

"Ten years ago," replied Aster. "Well, that's a long story." Aster shuffled across the old jute rug and sat by the window, chewing on his cigarette holder.

"Aunt Clare put tea and shortbread cookies on the table for you."

Aster wasted little time lifting the lid off the crystal cookie dish as Donovan poured the tea.

"So when can we begin?" asked Donovan.

Aster dunked his cookie. "First thing tomorrow morning, we'll get started. In the meantime, we can get to know each other. Perhaps you can tell me how you approach writing."

———

Donovan knocked on Aster's door. He had several manuscripts and a typewriter in his hands.

"Good. You've brought all your work. Most new writers are reluctant to show their work," Aster said. "Looks like you've been

busy, so let's get started."

Donovan sat at the desk, which overlooked the backyard. Aster pulled the armchair next to the desk and began to read. Donovan waited nervously.

"Okay," Aster said, putting down the pages. "I like the concept of your first story about the group of widows who love attending funerals. It's complex, quirky and subtly nuanced. But with a few changes, you can make this story more vivid."

The hours passed. Donovan worked on one story after another, while Aster sat near him, editing, re-editing and tossing the rejects into the wastepaper basket.

"Good work, son," Aster sighed, standing and stretching his legs. "You've really made progress. Tomorrow we can discuss how you develop your ideas. If I know a little more about your process, I can help you even more."

Donovan smiled and eagerly confirmed the next day's lesson. As he reached for the trash, Aster said, "Don't bother with that. Let me empty it—I need the exercise after sitting for so long."

The next day, Donovan again sat at the roll-top desk, carefully re-working another story, while Aster read, edited and gave him encouragement.

"I know it's difficult, but if you just write every idea that comes to you, you will find that line or two that makes it believable." Aster put his hand on Donovan's shoulder. "And you know the saying, anything worthwhile takes time and sacrifice."

Donovan nodded and kept pounding the keys of the old typewriter long into the night.

The third morning, when Donovan brought tea and cookies to Aster's room, the door was partially open and Aster was nowhere around. Donovan paused at the door before spotting Aster's open trunk, from which paper overflowed. Looking over his shoulder, he quickly went into the room and knelt by the trunk. As he read page after page, his familiarity with the words took him by surprise.

"I don't believe it," Donovan said disgustedly, sitting in the armchair and clutching the pages.

"I can explain," Aster said, walking softly into the room. He put the empty wastebasket next to the typewriter, sat across from Donovan, and took a cup of tea. "You wanted to know why I stopped writing, I believe?"

Donovan nodded.

"Writing is such an awful mess." Aster leaned back into the chair and crossed his legs. Heavy brown wingtips jutted from the frayed cuffs of his trousers. "If you want to be an original, challenging author, you have to come up with fresh ideas or have

some edge. It's hard. I have not had any success at it since the new technology—you know, computers and the like."

Donovan watched his reflection deaden in Aster's glasses. "I think I understand the first part of your statement, but you lost me with the rest."

Aster took a cookie from the plate. "When I was a young man, near your age, I had aspirations of becoming a writer. I had written my first adventure novel by the time I was twenty-two." He paused and rearranged his spongy frame in the chair. "It was rejected by every publishing house I sent it to. They all said, quite politely, that it had been done better by Raymond Chandler, Ernest Hemingway and James Michener."

"You must have really taken their comments to heart. Your two novels reminded me of Hemingway's style and Michener's characters."

"Someone once said, and I've forgotten who, that there are two keys to original ideas. The first is knowing where to find them, and the second is to never reveal them." The old writer dusted his mouth of crumbs with his handkerchief.

Donovan's face was expressionless. "I'm confused."

"You see, in my day, writers sat in their studies and cranked out page after page. Then, as they read their manuscripts, sipping on their wine or whiskey, they would toss what they did not like into the wastebasket. You see, no matter how good they were, invariably they weren't satisfied with what they wrote. And that's where I come in."

Donovan squirmed in the rigid chair across from Aster, waiting for him to make his point. And he did.

"I remembered what the publishers had told me and decided that I should meet some of the notable writers of the day—like Hemingway, Updike and the old bore himself, Michener. I even

tried visiting Maugham, but he was always traveling abroad." Aster scooted to the edge of his chair. "One day I saw Hemingway emptying his trash, and the idea hit me."

"You ripped them off!" Donovan gasped in disbelief.

"You'd be surprised how many good ideas authors throw away. The pickings were easy."

Donovan slumped in the chair, a gurgling sound rolled up from his belly. Aster flicked his eyebrows and smiled between bites of shortbread.

"So you never really knew them, just their trash bins? I can't believe I'm hearing this," said Donovan. "You've written two best-sellers. You've had accolades heaped on you. How did you man-age to do it?"

"It was pretty easy. Fitzgerald's trash was easy to get at, although the paper often smelled of bourbon. Updike played a lot of golf. A round of golf takes what, four or five hours—plenty of time to sift through the wastepaper," said Aster unashamedly.

"And the others?" Donovan's voice was barely audible.

"Equally easy. Hemingway fished a lot. Everyone had a rou-tine. H. G. Wells once said there is no passion in the world greater than altering someone else's draft."

"I don't think he was referring to what you did—or do," Donovan quickly replied.

"I just took it to its next logical step."

"So you have no remorse?"

"Remorse?" Aster pondered that while sipping his tea. "No. Maugham once was asked about the rules for writing. You know what he said?"

"No," hedged Donovan.

"That no one knows what they are!" Aster laughed softly.

"And now, with technology, the trash bins aren't as full as they once were?"

"Sad, isn't it? Today, everyone has a computer and paper shredder, or most everyone. About all I can find anymore are Visa bills and grocery lists."

Donovan shook his head. "But you still try?"

"Old habits die hard. I have a few things stored away," said Aster.

"So, this contest is a fraud, too?"

"Fraud is such an ugly word, but yes," answered Aster. "This is just a way to discover new talent, and new ideas so to speak. I look specifically for typewritten entries. I spotted yours right off. That way I don't have to worry about anything being erased with the touch of a key."

"So what you're teaching me is...?"

"Oh, my writing lessons are in earnest," Aster assured him.

Donovan looked at the steamer trunk in the alcove of the room. "So, how does it work? I show you my writing, tell you my ideas, you edit it, and then offer to empty the trash?"

"Essentially," frowned Aster. "It's much easier than spending months on end somewhere picking through rubbish. You know, I once spent eight months in a sleazy Texas motel so I could go through Michener's trash bins at night with a flashlight. That guy was right—Michener couldn't say hello in a chapter."

"It was six pages!" snapped Donovan. "I know that quote."

Aster just grinned. "More tea?"

"So, who was your last novel from?"

"*The Shred of Evidence* is an eclectic mix of early Stephen King, Danielle Steel and some odds and ends I collected in the good old days," replied Aster. "Hot, steamy sensuality with a touch of the grisly sells." Aster tilted his head and nodded toward the trunk. "You'll make a good writer. I can tell. You're curious, introspective and a good observer. I could teach you the tricks of the trade."

"No thanks," replied Donovan, firmly tucking the pages he had recovered from Aster's trunk close to his side. "Good or bad, I think I'd rather do it myself."

Aster let out a long sigh. "You're sure you're not interested? We've got enough material in there for five novels."

"Quite! I assume you'll be leaving in the morning, then?"

asked Donovan politely.

"Yes. I have another appointment."

"No doubt another first-prize winner?"

"Yes. Seattle is a dreary place, but there are a lot of promising young writers there." Aster anticipated Donovan's next question. "And no, I'm not afraid of being found out. Who'd believe it? Besides, everyone concerned is either dead or too self-absorbed."

Donovan hung his head as he collected the tea service and empty cookie plate.

"Keep writing," said Aster. "You really do have talent. All my first-prize winners do."

Donovan grimaced at the old man's words.

"And remember, if you get stuck with the next line of a story, just have two guys coming through the door, like Ray Chandler proposed."

"I thought he said two guys with guns!"

"The guns were my idea. I let him borrow that from me." Aster's belly began to bounce as he laughed.

McNeal and McGunnigan entered Haig's Bar grinning. "So how did the writing lessons go?" asked Itty. "Learn anything?"

Donovan paused. He stared down at a new book of matches, minus one, peering out of his shirt pocket. The smell of burnt paper still lingered on his fingers. "The lessons were invaluable," Donovan replied, pulling the matchbook out of his pocket and tossing it onto the bar.